THE HOUSE OF DeLANCRE

A stranger might think he'd stumbled on a cathedral built by the worshippers of a hundred different religions. There were signs and meanings nearly obliterated in their fusion of architectural design, but the latent forces remained incredibly powerful. Worlds within worlds, histories and mythologies merging and mating. Flying buttresses expanded out across neo-Roman ramparts. Three-tier elevation dropped off to two and hopped to castle-like cube stairways leading to four- and five-story towers. Basque and Romanesque styles melded with Gothic spires, and occasional dormers and gables faced into each other from across the open quad at the center.

Baroque stone and glass mounted the night surrounded by a canopy of gargoyles and other winged figures. Inside, rooms were shaped as hexagons, seals of Solomon, and pentacles, with many other chambers cut into the Sephiroth and Sephirah angelic symbols, other Kabbalistic sigils, ancients runes and swastikas. Corridors dead-ended one day and opened into living quarters the next. Windows had been calculated to throw shadows on the fields spelling out ancient prayers to gods only half-believed to be gone. Standing in those shadows on holy days could kill a man or drive him insane with a head full of barely heard whispers.

TOM PICCIRILLI

A
LOWER
DEEP

LEISURE BOOKS   NEW YORK CITY

For Michelle, for her faith and love,
and to Jack Cady, who understands the weight of history.

A LEISURE BOOK®

October 2001

Published by

Dorchester Publishing Co., Inc.
276 Fifth Avenue
New York, NY 10001

ISBN 0-8439-4921-X

Visit us on the web at www.dorchesterpub.com.

A
LOWER
DEEP

Which way I fly is hell; myself am hell;
And in the lowest depth a lower deep
Still threat'ning to devour me opens wide,
To which the hell I suffer seems a Heav'n.
                            —Milton, *Paradise Lost*

Part One

A Lower Deep

Chapter One

Despite the fiery omen of murder burning over their table, the couple seemed perfectly content. The woman's smile brought out the beautifully etched laugh lines around her eyes. Her lips parted to show a sexy, small overbite, and her dark hair glistened with melting snow. The husband stood a solid six feet, large scarred hands looming from inordinately thin wrists. They placed their infant son in a stroller between them and proceeded to laugh their way through appetizers. When the waiter named Jake arrived with their entrées, they shyly admitted it was their second anniversary. Fred and Kathy Rumsey introduced themselves and their son, Walt.

His voice booming with a two-pack-a-day smoker's resonance, Jake bellowed and offered complementary champagne. The couple thanked him but chose a chateau instead, their baby giggling affectionately. Jake returned and poured wine that oozed from the bottle like black clotted blood.

The Fetch-light spun over their table, whirling languorously before fading to a hazy nimbus of crimson. Flames drifted across Walt's face and he groped for the waves of red lapping at him. When his fingers touched it, the Fetch-light abruptly drew back like a startled animal and vanished. Walt started to scream.

I groaned, finished my steak, and took a last sip of beer.

Snow spattered against the windows in thick gouts while Kathy Rumsey quieted her child. Top-heavy trees leaned precariously, branches bogged like weary arms, and the surrounding fields were an empty range of wind and darkness. Downtown Billings, Montana, hadn't gone far in disproving the notion that this wasn't a nexus of social night life. I ordered coffee. Eidolons and shadows wove intricate patterns in the growing drifts surrounding the restaurant.

The dinner crowd left and the blizzard kept other potential patrons at home. Soon only the Rumseys, a few people at the bar, and I remained in the place. One woman in a black slit-skirt appeared to have been stood up by her date. The bartender looked uncomfortable giving her more to drink. Surrounding men joked loudly and paid for another round. They got giddier and became more and more hopeful with every swallow she took. Music played softly above their laughter, and timbers settling in the rafters sounded like occasional hammer blows coming from the roof.

The baby stared at me.

Jake opened the front door and glanced down the highway, muttering that he saw no traffic, not even the usual truckers working the long haul out of North Dakota. He perused the rest of us with a noncommittal grin, face flat at the thought of his poor tips tonight. His twin brother had recently been murdered: An astral afterimage followed limply behind him strung on a silver psychic wire, the dead part of his shared soul tumbling like a corpse being dragged. As Jake wandered back to the kitchen he brushed past the lady at the bar, who finished her drink, spun in her seat, and approached my table.

Her blond hair fell in a wild tangle about her shoulders, two sweeping curls crab-clawing into her mouth. Those dark eyebrows offset her features nicely. "Uhm—" she said. "Hey, listen—" Bleary green eyes scanned my coffee, the satchel at my feet, and the thin vase on the table filled with two freshly clipped ugly, half-dead wildflowers. Her gorgeous full lips were the kind that made men grimace in appreciation, that jaw set with a slight jut. "I'm Bridgett. Care to dance?"

The other guys grumbled and glared. They'd spent their money, cajoled, and bent an ear only to watch her walk off. This might not get bad but it probably would. Her dress hugged her abundant chest as well as all the other nice curves, and she threw a pose to make a few more show up. Bridgett knew just how to kick a step forward so one leg appeared like paradise from the slit-skirt, giving us all a slow view of the entire ride up her knee to midthigh. I hoped nobody was drunk enough to go for a rifle.

I told her, "Sure."

We made our way to the small dance floor at the other side of the room. She dropped heavily into my arms as we clumsily slow-danced to melodies that were hot before the Japanese surrendered. Snow continued to violently pound the windows behind us, battering the glass like frantic children dying to be let in. It felt good to hold a woman again, her nails scratching lightly at my back. There was a scent to her, one I hadn't smelled so strongly on another person in years. Church. It reminded me of my mother. Church in its truest, deepest form. The fragrance pervaded her pores. An energy of hymns, whitewash sermons, and an unshakable faith in the scriptures—but beneath that, something dank and awful.

She sobbed into my chest and murmured a name. Jerry. Terry, maybe. "So, I've got a question for you, okay?" She attempted to enunciate each word properly and did a pretty good job. "Why would a man not show up on the night he was supposed to make a surprise proposal except he talks too loud to his mother on the phone and let the secret out of the bag a few days ago?"

"Give the guy a break," I said. "There's a blizzard. Maybe he just got stuck on the side of a road."

"My ass! He's got a Dodge Big Red with a twenty-four-valve turbo diesel engine. I lent him the down payment. The thing could drive up Rushmore hauling two tons of cinder blocks." Bridgett suddenly dipped, jerking me to her. "Squeeze me," she whispered, and the provocative husky tone in there made my breath hitch. "Harder. I want you to hug me closer. Come on, at least let me feel you, if nobody else."

Moonlight still managed to ignite the flowing November sky as it grew more alive with the surging snowfall. The roughnecks who'd failed with Bridgett gave one last sneer in my direction before leaving. Maybe this would be all right. She slumped farther in my arms until I had to shift my grip on her waist to keep her from falling.

I caught another whiff of that blissfully sweet salvation and syrupy damnation church stink, and my second self trembled. He yipped a name I didn't quite recognize. I wondered how that odor came to be on her—whether Catholic school had invaded her life to such a great degree or her father was a Baptist preacher.

"You're a good dancer," she said as I shuffled and box-stepped. "You're wonderful at holding a woman."

I wasn't. I never had been, and my love Danielle had died because of it. Bridgett didn't look anything like Dani, but somehow I kept seeing hints of her and my brain began to twist. "Thanks, I appreciate the kind words."

She chuckled, a low and ugly sound. "I like your voice too. There's no saccharine in it, none of that haughtiness or twang either. You're not into trucks, are you? You got a place to stay?" For the first time a grin creased her face, one composed of annoyance and worry, and perhaps the thought of further humiliation. "You don't, do you? I see that pack on the floor. Huh, now isn't that something. I've got plenty of room." She leaned in close and tried to lick my neck, but she ended up on my collar. "I suggest you take me up on that offer. No matter where you're from, I can teach you things the girls don't do there at all, or at least not half as well."

The baby gazed about the restaurant with a cool reserve. Walt kept staring at me as his parents held hands and ate cheesecake. I worked Bridgett back into a nearby table just hard enough to knock its flower holder to the floor. Her heel crunched squarely on the oddly shaped wild roses, grinding them

19

into the carpet. "Hey, honey, watch where you're swinging me," she said. "I already made you the offer. No need to get pushy now."

"Sorry."

I braced her against the seat and stooped to check the roses, interpreting their position using a Romany version of phyllorhodamancy—divination through crushed flowers—and saw in the petals something about worshipers of toads, worms, and the gnawers of the dead.

The Rumseys gathered their toys, stroller, and diaper bag, and put Walt into his winter gear until he was packed up like a Power Ranger–loving Eskimo.

"Come on," I told Bridgett. "Let's go."

"Whoa, boy, you're a little slow out of the gate but you're a racehorse when you want to get moving. Give me a second here."

I left Jake a tip that would lighten his heart and when the psychic cord leading from the back of his head came around toward me I caught it in my concentration and snipped it with my mental teeth, allowing his dead brother's portion of their soul to at last let go.

Bridgett drew on a leather coat loaded with studs and buckles that clashed with her evening dress. She laughed humorlessly at nothing, grinning wildly and weaving with little excited steps as if imagining what her fiancé might do after finding us together in the morning. I pictured a guy in a large red truck backing over me a couple of times and it didn't put a smile on my face.

The parking lot was a blinding swirl of thrashing snow, and the few cars still remaining were almost buried by four-foot drifts. Rumsey carefully brushed off his station wagon.

"The blue Mazda's mine," she said. "It's not very practical in winter but I like it and . . . well, anyway—" She made a fluttery motion with her hand. "It's over there someplace, I think."

We got in just as Rumsey turned east onto the highway. It took me a minute or two to rock the Mazda out of its spot where the snow had bunched high around the tires. I followed at a fair distance with no other traffic in view. Bridgett kept trying to fondle me, still muttering about Jerry Terry, his Dodge, and broken promises. His mother would be pissed too—the old lady liked Bridgett and wanted grandkids soon before her bad hip completely gave out.

With her face planted in the side of my

throat, those lips were like passionate razors cutting deep that reminded me of another lady from the dead past. I put my arm around her and listened to her sighs, until at last she slept.

The Mazda handled poorly on the slippery highway, fishtailing and skidding all over. One headlight was out and the other pointed under the grille. I had trouble keeping Rumsey's station wagon in sight. We drove for twenty minutes before he pulled into a sparse hillside area and backed into a lengthy driveway, the house secluded by acres of brush on either side. I turned around and parked at the far edge of their property.

Even with the fierce wind blowing, a stench of blood and burned flesh bloomed over the house. Between that and the heady aroma of church I had barely enough time, as the nausea hit, to open the door and vomit outside the car. Spasms wracked me and I reached down to get a handful of snow and washed my face with it.

My second self uncoiled at the pungency in the air and pranced up my back. His mouth watered for bonemeal, Bridgett's sexuality, and the Fetch-lit doomed. Self nuzzled my neck, his tongue working at my skin the way Bridgett's never could, his breath warm in my ear and mind. He plucked at her coat, claws clinking rhythmically on the metal studs. *Hot-chee Mama. Nice winnebagos. Now you're thinking, boy!*

We've got problems.

He scrambled back and forth across the dash, his arousal overpowering. *Hey, no problem here!*

Finally he wheeled from her and splayed himself against the passenger window, sniffing and mewling. His eyes could pick up the Fetch-light glowing where mine no longer could, the flaming portent of murder spinning lazily in the night. Warmed in his blood lust, growls of ecstasy escaped him as he dreamed of what might be shuddering, pleading, or eviscerated inside. His thoughts pounded vindictively at me, showing images that made my already queasy stomach tumble further. Cold sweat exploded across my body. *Quit it.*

Good stuff going on in there, he said, *but weird.*

How so?

Can't tell yet.

You yipped a name before. What was it?

Did I?

I got out and left the car running, heater

going full blast to keep Bridgett warm. The woods were filled with tree branches so heavy with ice that they blocked my passage as I stumbled through hip-deep snow.

The first floor was brightly lit, every room blazing. Smoke rose from the chimney but no fire burned in the living-room fireplace. Two calico cats slinked across colonial furniture made by Sears. The Rumseys were nowhere to be seen. I tried the front and back doors and found them both dead-bolted. At the other side of the house, grades in the snow showed a few inches of shuttered windows at the stone foundation. I got on my belly and dug a corner of the shutter free, planted my feet, and pulled. The wood splintered and enough came away for me to see the painted black glass of a cellar. Self spat on the window and the paint on the inside bubbled and ran.

"Holy God," I whispered.

Self guffawed at the sight. *You've got to be kidding me. This? In Billings, Montana?*

Burning coals in a circular brick pit at the center of the cellar threw fingerlicks of shadow along the walls. A teenage girl lay gagged, naked, and tied spread-eagled to an old-fashioned metal box spring standing against one wall. Thin and gangly, her ribs pressed out sharply beneath her small breasts. It looked as if she'd been holed up here for at least a week. Intricate braids of lengthy red hair had come loose and curled down past the butterfly tattoo on her left thigh and the blackly emboldened name MEL on the right. She was covered with gashes, bruises, and burns from melted wax.

Gouged patterns of cabalistic symbols confirmed she'd never wear a bikini again. Copper wire had been strung so tightly around her wrists and ankles that the crusty skin had sealed over the wounds and her extremities had turned blue. She might not ever have the use of her hands or feet again. Self slurped and jitterbugged beside me, in his element now and wanting a taste of everything. He crooned, begging for entry. Mel—or Mel's girl—looked up. She spotted me and moaned, unsure of whether to cry out from beneath her gag, half expecting me to be just another form of agony.

At the opposite end of the basement, Fred and Kathy Rumsey sat in a poorly drawn chalk majik circle, a variation of Baphomet's inverted pentagram: The customary nine-feet of circumference had been

whittled to five, and titles of the Infernal hi-
erarchy had been misplaced between the
tetragrammaton of Jehovah's holy name
along the inner edge; along the outer ring
Hebraic figures at each point of the pentagram incorrectly spelled out *Corozon* instead of *Leviathan*.

The Rumseys wore cheaply sewn,
hooded gray robes, turning pages of a book
and reading aloud in badly accented
French. I recognized passages from the
eighteenth-century grimoire called *La Pe-
tite Grossetete* written by Emile la Duc, a
charlatan hoping to cash in on the depravity of certain French nobility of the time.
His wife had killed him with a broom handle.

Walt sat in his stroller, still silently staring.

If not for the girl, it would have been
laughable. Another couple of ridiculous
modern satanists, and poorly adept ones at
that, wearing Halloween costumes and
humping books on the occult back from the
library. Not too uncommon a sight in the
Manhattan or LA underground club scenes,
with parlor games, group sex, blood fetish,
and a modicum of Anton La Vey's *Satanic
Bible* special effects tossed in for good mea-

sure. Shops in Greenwich Village and on the Sunset Strip stocked eyes of newt and devil's chalices, catering to the social fringe. But . . . Christ, in Billings, Montana? None of this accounted for the signs I'd seen in the roses. The Rumseys weren't witches, only perverts, kidnappers, and possibly killers.

The two-sided blade Rumsey used proved to be a true *athame*—a witch's knife— sharply honed as he stood facing his wife from across the circle, chanting an invocation so garbled I couldn't make any sense out of it. They approached and kissed, taking turns pricking their wrists, licking the droplets, and smearing each other's face with blood. The flames wavered as a real hint of sex majik filled the room. I held my hand to the glass. Bursts of yellow sparks popped painfully around my fingers, and the girl writhed as though I'd scratched her. Walt continued watching. Nothing fit together.

Something's wrong, Self said. *You know what I mean?*

Yes.

This reminds me of . . .

Me too. Neither of us liked talking about the beginning.

His breath cracked the remaining paint.
I'm getting bad vibes. Let's get out of here.
No.
Quickly. Now.
First, the girl.
Forget her, we've already got one in the car!
I leaned back ready to smash the glass and
he hissed, *Do that shit and you're so dead,*
as if daring me. *Variant majiks are in mo-*
tion. She's no one to care about. Just bait, a
thing on the floor lying in the open trap.
You've got to let this debacle play out.

Fred Rumsey untied the teenager and
dragged her stumbling into the Baphomet
pentagram. She sobbed and struggled
wearily until he dumped her into the circle,
scuffing the chalk marks and erasing all-
important characters—her head cracked
against the floor and she fell over semicon-
scious and groaning for Mel. The arcana intensified until the hair at the back of my
neck crawled, electrified.

The Rumseys took off their robes and
continued sharing the knife, cutting at each
other's naked flesh, getting into it now,
wielding the blade high and drawing it
down fast and slicing, tittering all the while.
They dragged it deeply across bodies, first
one and then the other, politely handing the

sticky *athame* back and forth, soon chopping and slashing through muscle and bone.

They were insane and they had no real style. True masters at the art of mutilation would have frowned at the waste. Their blood arched and splashed madly across the room. With a final thrust Fred Rumsey shoved the blade into his wife's heart—as she grinned and mumbled, giving up one last bark of delight—then turned the knife on himself, and with a careful flick opened his carotid. He dropped heavily over his wife, and their blood pooled across the pentagram and ran around the girl. It was only going to get worse.

"Enough of this crap."

I kicked in the window and dropped inside, the storm following as Self jabbered in the snow, the trap closing. Walt drooled and shook his head happily at me, arms filled with toys. I pulled his stroller out of the way. In the pentagram the Rumseys' corpses vibrated, eyes bulging and blinking, teeth bared.

Invisible daggers flayed them as I watched, skin ripping back from bone. Veins, nerves, and organs danced little shimmies as the viscera smoked, yanked free from the bodies like corn being shucked. Coagulating, the blood withdrew, and all that spineless flesh slid across the floor and began merging into one large mass that hunched before the teenager like a giant toad.

Get the girl, I said.

Nuh-huh, I'm not stepping into that screwy circle. You don't know her or owe her anything. She's got no character, no soul you can see. Why do you keep doing this? You can't care about her.

I just—

You don't, no one does. She's only meat on the floor, intended for the moment. She doesn't mean anything.

Shut up already.

Will you ever listen?

Nothing else to do but get it done. Conjuring Babylonian wards of protection—head back and arms out, pinkies precisely placed to cover the lifelines of my palms—I crossed the outer boundary of the Baphomet circle. Connecting with it was like tying into a conduit of fathomless anguish—and an overwhelming love of that anguish—as red mist reared about me.

Jaws of the corpses dropped open and cackled as the charnel beast formed of their flesh started sprouting heads now. Three semihuman, insectoid faces sprang from the belly of the eight-foot toad. Two pairs of arms extended from its viscous torso, those chitinous heads excitedly stirring. I picked up Mel's girl and backed away, feeling the majik trying to chew my skin off too. I dragged her outside the pentagram and wondered if running would do me any good.

Is that Arioch? I asked.

Yes, Self said, much calmer now than he should've been. That meant running wasn't going to work. A smile tugged his lips apart. *The Bishop of Worms. I haven't seen it since the goblin market in Sepharvain.*

Maybe you can reminisce.

An ally of thoughtful Adramelech, Chancellor of Hades, Keeper of the Wardrobe. Watch out for the wings. It doesn't use them for flying.

Get over here and help me.

I am here and helping you, Self said. *I always am.*

Arioch. Impossible—these simpleton satanists couldn't have called Lord Arioch from its sixty regions. I scanned the badly drawn chalk circle again for signs of hidden names of power, a subliminal command-

31

ment of the Infernal, or some obscure or coincidental incantation of the Light-bringer's echelon. I couldn't spot anything. The Bishop of Worms hopped forward with great scraping noises, four flaming hands stuffed with killing strokes.

Every eye on those three heads gazed at me in fury, each mouth working at once. Its voice contained multitudes, composed of the voices of half a million human and animal souls—I heard kids and women in there, dogs, cattle, and impaled ravens, the elderly evil and misbegotten, wailing beyond its words.

"And so," it said. "Am I a piece to be moved about in mortal games now, Necromancer?"

"There's been a mistake. I have no quarrel with you, Prince Arioch."

Something like a snicker—myriads of whines and yelps—escaped its throats. Razor-sharp wings sprouted from its sides, expanding to the entire width of the cellar and leaving gouges in the stone walls, buzzing as those four hands worked spells I couldn't comprehend. "I'll not be party to your gambit."

"I—"

"Why have you tried my patience so? You

and your brethren need to be made an example."

"My brethren?"

"You've finally called forward your death, children of oblivion."

"Now you're just being mean," I said. Black flames of hexes filled my own fists, motes of energy rising to encircle my eyes. "I didn't call you at all." In the back of my mind Self pleaded with me to leave the girl and make a dash for it, knowing I wouldn't.

"You are the impetus for this travesty, and for that alone I shall set a quarter region of Pandemonium aside for you." Twelve thousand torturers reserved throughout eternity, just for me.

Kathy Rumsey's features had been taffy-pulled along Arioch's back, widened ten times farther, but those laugh lines and that cute overbite were still plainly visible. Arioch appraised me, and I could sense the ego within the Bishop of Worms. As slayer of a hundred thousand Arab soldiers in the deserts of Medain Sali, next in line as Chancellor of Hades, he did not act without prudence. I spun mystic litany webs about the room hoping to hold it back long enough to get the infant and teenager out. Why had it mentioned my brethren?

Tom Piccirilli

"Give me a life and I'll leave this damnable plane for the moment, in peace," Arioch said in all its conflicting voices. "Settle your own debts. You can afford no less."

"You've taken two lives already."

"Voluntary husks tender no pleasure, nor payment."

In a fashion, the Bishop of Worms was right. An Infernal of his stature asking—not even commanding anymore, but asking—for a single life was an incredibly polite gesture. Offering to depart without further murders proved a testament to Adramelech's influence. Even in hell chancellors were devout on keeping peace.

"How about a couple of cats?" I asked.

A maelstrom of baying and shrieks immediately crammed the basement. Arioch's many faces and fingers and teeth pointed at me. "I'll have the maimed female child now, for further disfigurement, or you condemn and forfeit ten others to me."

Do it, do it, Self urged from the window. *It'll all work out . . . don't put yourself through this anymore. This isn't your burden or trial.*

It's mine and yours too.

Will you trust me for once?

Like hell.

34

"Sorry," I said to a prince of hell. "Still no good."

Arioch's three heads opened in frustration, mandibles and pincers snapping as loudly as clashing swords. It straggled forward and cried, "Your damnable kind does not deny me!"

I pulled back my arms and drove hexes straight into its middle face, black and fiery spells pouring off its cheeks in splashes of flame and embers. The weight of history is always upon us. Words ran roughly over my lips in the same way the Knights Templar sang during the Crusades, before the Bishop of Worms orchestrated King Philip IV of France's condemnation of the order. Hundreds of the knights took their mystical secrets to the stake. That voice of screams split apart, and among the separate screeches I heard my dead enemies, inhumanly thin whispers, and Grand Master Templar Jacques de Molay's curses as he burned.

Malevolence slithered in there pretending to be Danielle.

She said, "Come for me. Find me, love."

I lunged as jagged green and blue charges of arcana flashed between us. Those incredibly sharp wings whizzed over my head, hunting to slash through my neck. Its blazing arms caught me flush in the chest and my teeth slammed together on my tongue.

Arioch said, "You've much to learn."

"Don't I know it." I coughed, grimacing, and trying to put my burning shirt out.

Its hands dimmed, the unknown incantations skittering about the room, cold and impenetrable. Those arms grabbed me and changed beyond color to the distorted silver of a mirror. Prince Arioch hauled me into the air, hungry to add my flesh to its transient body, but I managed to frantically kick free.

I flew backward into the corner and felt something crack hideously in my lower back. I drew breath to scream and the Bishop of Worms yanked Walt out of his stroller and pressed the child's mouth over mine.

Get over here, damn you!

Shhh, I am, Self said.

Visions clashed with memories and my brain came apart in shreds.

She was there, my love, alive in my arms—in the past, where we swung out of the parking lot at the prom and headed for the pond, and impossibly in the near future. The coven circled us as always, acting on their own delights in the old covenstead, lost in common depravity, with the priests shivering behind their pews again. Breath of God filled my lungs and launched into my mind. Eyes rolling back into my skull, the pure yet hazy breach of the future tinged my laughter with shrieks. Walt dropped off my face like a bloated spider.

I rolled, trying not to think, pressing the visions away as the skeletons of the Rumseys clattered together in a bedlam of ancient unholy tunes. Flopping forward, I rolled into the Baphomet pentagram tasting blood and chalk as Arioch laughed a thousand snickers and guffaws, not all of which were disgusting. The Bishop of Worms lifted its bulk to smash my spine, that stolen toad meat returning to color and hopping high against the ceiling to shatter timber.

Snow wafted in through the broken window, dappling the dead. I rose to my knees, thinking, She'll be with me again somehow, and I felt bones in my chest grating horribly. Flickering arcana swirled about the cellar like leaves in the wind. I called, *I could use a little help* and heard echoes of Persian oaths and chewing sounds. My vision swam and I couldn't find Self. Faces of Arioch made *tsk*ing noises like a disappointed father needing to punish a child further. Others *tsk*ed within it as well, Danielle's plaintive cries ringing through clearly. "My love."

"Stop it!" I shouted. My hexes whirled and picked up speed slinging through the air, winding in faster and faster until they struck with a burst of putrid yellow liquid and hissed steam, igniting that skin.

Graveyard musk spilled from the Bishop of Worms, an intoxicating mix of jasmine, fried hair, and souls frying. Arioch bellowed, the wing and arms on its left side torn off. Unable to stand, I finally focused on Self and saw him nibbling something, with ropes of fat trailing down his chin. He gave one last crunching champ of his fangs, smiled beatifically, and scrambled to me.

Scorching and sinewy, Arioch's fury was palpable, the oppressive fetor of carnage thickening around us until Self bopped in front of the prince of sixty regions and said, *Hey, Chief, got a minute to spare?*

Now a few puzzled gasps gurgled up within that dreaded voice. Arioch responded with a string of damnations. Danielle wept, "Come for me, love," and my throat closed. Eventually Arioch's three sets of pincers drew into repulsive displays of humor. Self spoke quietly, doubled over giggling at times, and clasped a reassuring arm around the grotesque toad. His claws caressed the Bishop of Worms' oozing flesh, and he occasionally licked the wounds I'd inflicted.

I could see the sweat fall from my second self's upper lip, those curved fangs beaming but ready to rip if necessary. At least I hoped so. Arioch nodded gravely, and moaned when Self's tongue touched a particularly sensitive area. It snorted in my direction and said, "You've strained my armistice with mortality further this night, Necromancer. Many will eventually perish in your stead. Think upon that with your human conscience, at what you've seen and have yet to live and suffer. I will take ten lives presently, and mention your name to their ghosts so that they might find you."

Mouths still frozen open in that threat, its chitinous heads dissolved from the top to the bottom, those blended organs and tissues now discarded and melting as Arioch's essence fled. Stretched but nearly whole, the Rumseys' skins draped sideways across their skeletons before liquefying into a puddle of viscous ooze.

You two are friends? I asked. The pain had me trembling badly.

It owed me from the Goblin Market, and has learned to pay its debts. It had a fling with my mother and I didn't tell its wife.

Why not?

He didn't answer. Certain secrets continued to be kept, boundaries uncrossed, although I could never be sure which were his and which could be mine.

Self uttered a low chuckle that drove deep, making me squirm even more as the agony in my back corkscrewed up through my brain and skewered it. He sprang and caught Walt's body by the neck, claws spearing that chubby belly, tearing as he ate, and then climbed inside the shell. *Relax, the kid was already long dead*. Walt unwound layer by layer like his parents, the child's corpse leaking dark goblin ichor. The dead baby had actually been used as a disguise. For a djinn.

No wonder the breath of God had been upon me. Djinn learn the future by eavesdropping on the angels, but why had Arioch damned me in this fashion?

Why was I destined to meet my brethren once more?

"So," I hissed. "It's been a game the whole time."

This stinks big time. We've been set up to take the heat. He said it as if he was enraged, but I could tell the fun and excitement was there too.

Crawling, I tried to grab hold of the wall and haul myself up, but I couldn't make it to my feet and slid facedown against the cold stone floor, groaning. I'd bitten through my tongue and my mouth filled with blood. Self wouldn't budge, continuing to maul and wash himself in the boy's remains, until I couldn't fight the pain anymore and was forced to ask.

Please help me, I begged.

But of course.

It had come to this before, the acknowledgment of need. I always hated seeing that grandiose look in his eyes, the arrogant smile so similar to my own. Is this what my love had seen in me? Self said, *I'm here*. He climbed out of Walt's chest and clambered across my shoulders, tore open my shirt, and lovingly licked and kissed my shattered back, claws prodding away the agony like acupuncture.

His invocations were in different archaic languages every time, as if he didn't want me to learn them. I moaned in relief, his palms gently massaging ruptured muscle. He kept thinking of what he wanted to do to Mel's girl, as if I might consider rewarding him with more blood. He stuck a pinkie into my mouth and scratched at my tongue until it fused together. Vertebrae and slipped discs audibly snapped back into place while I held in more screams, his healing hands and love mending me.

Thanks.

Always my pleasure.

When I could function again I brought the girl upstairs. I laid her on the couch in the living room and bundled her in crocheted blankets, untied the copper wires, and did my best to massage circulation back into her limbs. Maybe with a lot of therapy her hands and feet wouldn't be a total loss. Her breathing was shallow and erratic, heartbeat somewhat arrhythmic. Highly stylized sigil scars and glyph burns would forever mark her for other attentive demons to notice, but she'd make it for now. Using the phone in the kitchen I dialed 911 and left the receiver off the hook.

Self danced down the hallway to the bedroom and cried, *Yowzah! What's with the penguin?*

Bridgett sat on the bed dressed in a nun's full habit, with the cats curled in her lap, drinking a White Russian.

No wonder she'd smelled of church. I should've recognized it from the start but I'd fought too hard to forget. God's breath told me I was going back. Her leather coat had been thrown over a settee near the door. I touched it and it was dry. She'd been in the house the entire time.

She wore her habit the way folks at costume parties wear their clothes from the 1970s—as kitsch. Bridgett lifted her glass in a toast, gave an utterly false sloe-eyed gaze, and patted the covers beside her. "You did quite well," she said. "I think you deserve a reward."

Self clapped happily and said, *Thanks, baby, I knew I could count on you!* The beauty of blasphemy and depravity drove him nearly out of his gourd.

I grabbed her by the wrists and yanked her to her feet until our noses touched. "So you're the real executor behind tonight's display."

She laughed in my face until the killing hexes seeped from my hands. "Hey now," this wife of God novitiate said. "None of that."

"Who are you?"

"Very admirably handled. Apparently going rogue hasn't diminished any of your skills. We weren't altogether sure you'd survive the encounter with Prince Arioch."

I knew who she meant when she said "we" and I sucked the last drops of blood from my torn tongue down my throat, enjoying the taste.

Under her skirts skittered her familiar. Rosary beads bounced as the demon climbed up her chest to suck at her witch's teat, a tiny misshapen nipple near her collarbone. Colorless fluid dripped from her teat as the familiar finished feeding and worked its way out of the garments to sit on the brim of her habit, kissing those luscious lips. It cocked its head at me, crimson eyes glazed, with a smile that twisted with a hundred curved teeth.

Self yipped that name again and now I recognized the word: Thummim. An icy shiver worked up into my hairline.

Self said, *Mom?*

Bridgett's jawline jutted even farther, showing off the sweet angle of her neck. That juicy mouth kept trying to draw me in like Baphomet. The migraine hit at once, white-hot spikes driving into my forehead.

I let out a grunt and she grinned. "Jebediah sent me, but you already know that. Your days as a solitary are at an end. He wants you back and the new coven isn't complete without you. We need our Master Summoner. Say yes and we'll help you raise that bitch Danielle from the dead."

Chapter Two

Somewhere between Mullen and Lincoln, Nebraska, tooling east into the dawn on the dark expanse of I-73, Brenda Hasselman pulled her eighteen-wheeler *Blue Moon* iron box sharply into a truck stop.

Six diesel islands lay as empty as the four hundred miles and half dozen weigh stations beforehand. She said, "Listen, if you don't start making a little conversation soon I'm gonna boot your ass out right here. And believe me, this coffeepot called Myra's Home Cookin' ain't the place to find yourself thumbing at five in the morning. Myra's real name is Freddy Calhoun and once he starts talkin' about Oswald you got to hear it all. The Mafia, Monroe, Ruby and the Mexicans, KGB, and how it was LBJ himself really up in the book depository. This is the last stop for me until I slide into Aurora and get my six hours' sleep. I'm not asking for a life story, y'understand, but I'm not especially fond of silence. Reminds me of my tight-lipped ex-husband. That man couldn't string a simple sentence together between two cans of beer."

With ratty sneakers and oily duck hunter neon jacket, Brenda Hasselman cut anything but an imposing figure even inside her own Kenworth cab. She drove wearing huge gloves that made her look like a little girl dressed in her father's clothes. She had a kind but aggressively high pitched voice that brought derisive comments from the night radio chatter every time she picked up the mike.

She had the mark of fire on her forehead, the touch of Iblees, king of the Djinn. Jebediah and the others took great pride in matters of detail and had already set my course. I either fought or followed, and the breath of God allowed me the advantage of already knowing what I would do. Brenda Hasselman was just another part of the fetch, a way to see me home again.

She shut off the engine. "You better be well versed in the magic bullet theory. You sure are the weirdest son of a bitch I've met in my last four runs. Not quite as fucked-up as the honcho who wanted to sit naked on the roof of the cab and sing 'Hail Columbia' but you got a few knots. You and Freddy Calhoun'll get along just fine."

We were six days from the full moon. The next major sabbat wouldn't be until the Feast of Lights, Oimelc, on February 2, and the next minor not until the winter solstice of December 22. Bridgett was almost certainly the Maiden of the Coven, and she'd clearly been tutored in Jebediah's melodramatic style.

"So, you gonna talk or not?" she asked.

"I'm not," I said.

She stared at me for a long time, the touch of djinn marring her otherwise pale and soft face. "I had that feeling. Okay, forget I asked. Good luck to you."

"You too."

I scanned the truck stop and spotted a middle-aged man coming out of the diner with two Styrofoam cups of coffee. He looked tired and I offered to drive and pay part of the gas. He didn't even bother to look me up and down. "Okay," he said. "Sounds good to me."

"I appreciate it."

His forehead burned with the scrawl of Iblees, who had been created out of fire, grown with the angels, and ruled the world before Adam. In refusing to bow before man he had been cast aside like Lucifer. "Where you headed?"

I started his car and said, "Church."

Power of God, murder, and death resisted time. At the edge of the covendom—a radius of three miles from the temple at the center of Jebediah's estate—sat the ruins of the church, half hidden in the snowbound, overgrown thickets.

The belfry appeared scarred by lightning, and two of the three bells lay in the dirt and ice, the third precariously balanced on the rotted cedar shingles of the peak. Birds, animals, and men had nested here in previous winters. Most of the pews and railings had been piled into the middle of the altar for a bonfire, but only been used little by little over the years. Several of the small, stained-glass windows were boarded over but the huge gaping holes in the ceiling remained, with snow wafting about in the shadows.

The crucifix hung by only its bottom bolt, the cross askew but not inverted, hanging sideways. People like the Rumseys would have thought you'd need to pray to Satan bowing before a black altar, chanting scripture backward, stepping on the holy wafer, and committing sodomy in the pulpit in order to be a witch. That's why they had been used so easily, blind without any form of truth to follow except one based on ridicule of Catholicism; and so the power remained with Catholicism.

Cotton Mather had gotten it wrong again when he wrote, "The witches do say that they form themselves much after the manner of Congregational Churches." The mocked have the strength of the martyred.

Moonlight beat down, and the walls looked as though they'd sweated blood.

The pew where I'd held Dani while she died had been smashed for kindling. I scrawled fiery symbols in the air and the wood lit with the flaring, golden smudges of her murder. I dug through the debris and held the splintered section of stained wood to my chest and wept like a madman, as if she were still with me.

The dust and layers of years peeled back one after the other, down to the marrow of my life. Her blond hair splayed against my thigh, some of the curls torn out by the roots, other patches black and fried. Her broken nose and torn face ran red over my lap.

I'd had to fight back thoughts of resurrection. She coughed and gagged my name, and we whispered the prayers we'd learned in Sunday school together as shrieks echoed for miles across the covendom, the rest of our brethren dying. I kissed her gently, covered with the bite marks of my father, and even in those last moments she sought to soothe my sorrow. Her mouth moved, making plaintive, affectionate sounds. My second self kept his claws to her throat, feeling the pulse steadily fade. I would have relinquished every ounce of majik I'd possessed if only Archangels Michael and Gabriel and the other Cherubim would have held back Azreal from his course as the angel of death. Danielle sputtered blood and tried to smile while I begged forgiveness, and her broken fingers reached for my cheek.

Azreal sneaked beneath my hands and took my love from me.

Give it a rest, Self said. *You're stuck in a rut, always living out this same moment.*

Break free, leave her where she lies. Go with the penguin. You just need to get laid. Forget about her already.

Say that again.

What?

Say it again.

He blinked and licked his lips. He scurried forward, climbed my shirtfront, hugged me, and moaned.

The mocked have the strength of the martyred.

It was like Jebediah to leave the church standing, willfully disregarding it, repressing the reality of that last night in an attitude of dismissal. To raze it would have been an acknowledgment, and any acknowledgment would have been considered defeat.

He'd been slow in gathering the new coven, much more patient than I would have expected. Ten years making the careful correct choices, whatever he thought they might be. Bridgett proved to be a perfect underling for his consideration. There were many mad and sacrilegious nuns, but few were as beautiful.

I worked through the thickets on an uphill grade, past the pine and sage and several varieties of hazel. Snow burned with the witching moon. I fought through the brush until I broke into the open fields. I approached from the northeast, the symbolic dividing line between the cardinal point of hell's north and the righteous east, and I found a hundred-foot length of wrought-iron spike fencing unconnected to anything else, barring my way.

A gate swung wide a few yards farther on. Once it had been called the devil's door, traditionally opened after baptisms to let demons and original sins escape. Jebediah used it to force the coveners to walk the powerful northern path. It was merely another symbol of darkness, but one grounded in true faith. Jebediah and I had spent years quarreling over such tokens and trivia of belief. It's why I was still alive.

Instead of entering through the gateway I climbed the twelve-foot-high fence and kept heading northeast on as straight a trail as I could.

Until I finally came home to the House of DeLancre.

A stranger might think he'd stumbled on a cathedral built by the worshipers of a hundred different religions. There were signs and meanings nearly obliterated in their fusion of architectural design, but the latent forces remained incredibly powerful. Worlds within worlds, histories and mythologies merging and mating. Flying buttresses expanded out across neo-Roman ramparts. Three-tier elevation dropped off to two and hopped to castlelike cube stairways leading to four- and five-story towers. Basque and Romanesque styles melded with Gothic spires, and occasional dormers and gables faced into each other from across the open quad at the center.

Baroque stone and glass mounted the night surrounded by a canopy of gargoyles and other winged figures. Inside, rooms were shaped as hexagons, seals of Solomon, and pentacles, with many other chambers cut into the Sephiroth and Sephirah angelic symbols, other cabalistic sigils, ancient runes, and swastikas. Corridors dead-ended one day and opened into living quarters the next. Windows had been calculated to throw shadows on the fields spelling out ancient prayers to gods only half believed to be gone. Standing in those shadows on holy days could kill a man or drive him insane with a head full of barely heard whispers. Other secret areas could only be reached by climbing certain roofs and ascending ladders from the outside.

Solomon had commanded the djinn to complete David's temple, and according to the Bible there was neither hammer, nor axe, nor any tool of iron heard in the house while it was building. Now that Jebediah had mastery over Iblees, the djinn had continued work on the estate.

Scars remained though, despite the years of rebuilding. Cracks in the foundation, rips across the stone buttresses as if massive talons had scraped and scrabbled for purchase, and tattered chunks of roofing where the House of DeLancre would never again heal.

Pierre answered the door.

The weight of centuries stooped his shoulders and smeared his features across his face like an insect wiped against a pane of glass. His lips nearly drooped off his chin, his Adam's apple nestled so deeply in his chest that it bulged far below his collar. His eyes were so empty that they appeared flat and black as shale.

Dust covered Pierre's bleached flesh, hair, and butler's suit almost as though he'd been laid aside in a closet and only recently brushed off and returned to the world. He would never play the lute again. Too many portions of his soul had been flung far and wide.

Here was the progenitor of the DeLancre family.

At first, a decade ago, I'd believed him to be a reincarnate—a soul trapped by the sins of his sadistic reign over the Basque. Pierre deLancre presided as a witch-trial judge in France and sent six hundred people to the stake. He compiled accounts of alleged activities at sabbats.

As a lawyer he'd been obsessed with uncovering criminal activities, and in 1609 he was ordered by Henry VI to deal with witches supposedly plaguing Labourd. The Basques were a mysterious people, mostly sailors who spent months on journeys to Newfoundland, leaving their women to run the villages. Superstition ran high in such a people who upon the men's return would have unbridled feasts, drinking and dancing wildly according to their customs. DeLancre was fascinated with them, and like all witch-hunters his tortures caused mass confessions and implications. He relied primarily on the testimony of children, some of whom testified against their own parents. He played the lute while the faggots burned, and he ordered condemned girls to dance around the immense fires before their own executions.

He'd raped dozens of women and a number of them had survived. Those who were not witches made pacts with the Infernal and became so in order to have justice. His own children had bound him to their lineage and flayed his ghost, and he'd been passed on from generation to generation like the ashes he should have been.

My second self unfurled from around my neck and leaped. *Pierre, my man, how things been?* Self gave him a wet kiss on the cheek, then sauntered into the hallway. He stared back at me over his shoulder appraising my expression.

I couldn't read exactly what had gone on with his mother and Arioch, or just whose side he would be on when the taking of sides would again be in question. He fidgeted with ecstasy, all those fangs on view in his looming smile, as the cathedrals of the world opened before us. He ran down the corridor squealing. I wondered what I would be without him, if anything at all.

Pierre held his arm out to take my satchel and coat but I waved him off. Jebediah kept the dead like house pets. He enjoyed staring into their eyes and sending them off on meaningless tasks. He dressed them in jesters' costumes and French maid outfits, orangutans and conquistadors, and then invited the wealthy and affluent of the city to masques and costume balls. How he used to laugh when the witches and the murdered danced with the mayor and councilmen and the debutante sixteen-year-old daughters of celebrities.

There was a time Jebediah had sent my own father for me, my dad's shoes on the wrong feet.

Pierre stared at me without expression and said, "Welcome home, most gifted Master Summoner." Even Arioch's voice sounded more human. Pierre DeLancre's hatred of witches had been fanatical in life, and it had grown even worse in the impotence and despair of his resentful, feeble existence. Not many demons had eyes so virulent and ruthless as those of bitter men.

I brushed by him. "Never address me that way again."

"As you wish."

"Where is he?"

"Master DeLancre is in the library."

I walked for ten minutes before realizing that the djinn had moved the library intact to a different section of the manor. This proved to be another game, allowing me to wander lost in Jebediah's sanctum. It showed how much things had changed, and how substantially they remained fixed in a separate hell.

I passed arched and vaulted ceilings, immense stairwells, and open banquet tables where a century ago sovereign rulers licked the convulsing feet of their servants. Self said, *This is getting a tad annoying*. He licked my finger and drew his bottom teeth down against my wrist hard enough to draw a few drops of blood. I held my palm out and recited a passage from the *Nis Kati*. Suddenly there was a heavy charge in the air as a draft moved against my face. I looked at my hand and rivulets of my blood flowed upward into my palm in a series of lines, laying out a map for me to follow to the library.

Spirits walked at all hours down the gnarled passages and stairwells. Occasionally one of the Basque women tortured to death by Pierre would drift into the edge of my peripheral vision only to vanish when I glanced over. Other dead sat under furniture and wept or laughed as I moved against the wheels of the labyrinth, passing from one cathedral to the next. Various ancient gods stretched out on the walls. A short corpse dressed in the rags of a tuxedo clambered up the chains of a chandelier and peered down. It took me a moment to recognize him as a former governor who'd died without signing a proposed cut in Jebediah's tax bracket. The frivolity of necromancy.

Depending on which chamber we passed, Self grinned, frowned, or hugged my knee and trembled. *We've forgotten too much about this place. There are more puzzles and enigmas now.*

Yeah.

No music here the way it was, no real fun, not a hell of a lot left to make a good impression.

It was never any fun.

Black puddles and bone splinters ran beneath doors. *Must be the reincarnate maid's day off.* Not all hexes soothed. Some prayers could still carry weight long after the devoted had made their pacts. Above, distant shrieks echoed across time and place. Perhaps someone was being sacrificed at this hour or decades in the future or centuries ago, here or in another country where the brutalities of the world moved against anyone who went bare chested or spread poultices on wounds instead of leeches.

Eventually we stood before the library door. Self tongued the doorknob, tasting the ages of arcane knowledge within. Filaments of protective spells had been woven across the portal, more like a bell than any measure against intruders.

Self said, *Luc-eee, I'm hooo-ome* and snapped the charm. He kicked out and the door swung open.

I had to stamp down the old excitement. My breath hitched as I looked about the large room and saw just how much the DeLancres' collection of artifacts and lore had grown. The djinn had done a good job at expanding the library. It was three times its previous size and still didn't have quite enough room to fit all the occult tomes the family had amassed in nearly four hundred years.

Thousands of volumes and acquisitions filled the shelves and tables: talismans, amulets, fetishes, dolls, athames, and other blades, chalices, white, red, and black candles, bone carvings, instruments of torture, and devices I couldn't quite fathom. Pierre's lute rested on a hickory stand beside a fist-sized rock taken off the corpse of Giles Corey, who'd been crushed beneath stones by his Salem neighbors for refusing to plead innocent or guilty to witchery. When ordered to confess Corey had simply shouted, "Add another stone." He'd been a personal hero to both Jebediah and me, for different but not quite opposite reasons.

More souls had been sold in the procuring of this horde of arcane goods than there were words on all the pages.

Papyrus and codex from the great library of King Assurbanipal, emperor of Assyria, lined the walls in glass cases. Jebediah's strongest conjurings had gone into the guarding and defenses of these chambers. Mystic shields defended all this history, wisdom, and doctrine.

Locked in iron sheaths remained Babylonian books such as *Maklu*, the burning; *Utukki Limbuti*, these evil spirits; *Labartu*, the hag demon; and *Nis Kati*, the raising of the hand. Resting side by side with flesh-bound grimoires were the original missing books of the Bible, including the War of the Lord and the 114 Sayings in the Gospel of Thomas. Here lay Solomon's Theurgia Goetica, which he'd used to annoy Arioch. In one corner rested a replica, or perhaps the original, copper cauldron in which King Solomon had imprisoned the djinn. And beside it was the Torah as it was meant to be read, the five books without breaks of paragraph, sentence, or even words—comprising the one true name of God.

The knowledge, pleasure, and power here could drive any man insane.

And in the center of it all sat Jebediah DeLancre.

Chapter Three

His hair had grown back salted with white, and his lips had mended imperfectly. The upper lip tugged hard to the left so that a shard of his yellow canine would always be partially exposed in a delighted sneer. One eyebrow was mostly missing, a dark stretch of burn scar replacing it. He looked twenty pounds thinner, nearly gaunt, with his cheeks covered in blue shadow and his chin now a bony point with the barest smidgen of a goatee. He'd always had a nervous habit of plucking at it while he talked to men he was about to kill.

If he knew I was here, then he paid no attention. At his desk, he pored over a small pile of dirt, inspecting and combing through it with a letter opener. He divided the earth into lines—first horizontal, then vertical, and diagonal, realigning them over and over. His familiar, Peck in the Crown, had been purified and accepted to heaven by one of the lowest Sephiroth angels minutes before Dani had died. Peck in the Crown could never be replaced after its redemption. Now Jebediah, despite the awesome amount of arcana at his service, seemed less than half the man he'd once been, betrayed by his beloved familiar. His glare forever held righteous hatred and incredible overconfidence, but loss and transgression tinged his eyes as well.

That final night I'd prayed that Jebediah would be dissuaded from his left-hand path and join the monks of Magee Wails Island, the way his brothers had. Only Uriel and Aaron possessed the gifts needed to keep him in check. The tolerance and patience and tenacity to resist most manners of temptation.

Afterward, when I'd curbed the infection of my father's bites, buried Dani, and laid out the charms to keep anyone from toying with her remains, I'd kneeled before her tombstone and couldn't even cry. The grave had never seemed so warm.

There are times when the future is more obvious than the present; our pain and rage and separate fates couldn't coexist. Jebediah and I could not escape each other. Both of us were damned, but one's damnation would have to be forfeited to the other. I'd known that the day I'd met him.

He smoothed the dirt on his desk and wiped his hands, looked up, and said, "Hello."

The anticlimax of the moment rocked me. We stared at each other and a lost lifetime of loathing flooded my skull. Self clapped and shuffled a two-step, digging the images running through my thoughts. The migraine and memories drove down like spear thrusts and I wondered why the hell I was still alive.

Jebediah stood and made a weak gesture of greeting, a half-formed attempt to shake my hand, or perhaps he was going to try to hug me. Revolted, I gagged and spun aside. He grinned as if we should talk about high school and football games, old movies, and recent best-selling novels. My heart rate doubled and the cold sweat streaked my back. My fingers twitched like crazy.

He said, "Welcome home."

My jaw dropped and I choked out baby noises, the hexes suddenly pouring from me, black sparkling motes rising to my eyes, fists burning. So much horror stood between us that I could almost see a violent red ocean rising over our feet. He stepped away, amusement playing beneath that sneer. I said something but didn't quite hear what it was. I said it again and missed it again. He cocked his head, puzzled. Finally I understood what I was asking him.

"Why?"

It was a stupid question.

He smiled, that jagged sliver of tooth as pointed as a needle. "I need you. We've finally come full circle."

"You have. I just wanted to be left alone."

"That's never been a possibility, no matter how much you desire it. We're a covenant. You made a vow to be one with us. Despite my studies you remain the Master Summoner. My summoner."

"Our vows are hardly sustaining or enduring. There is no coven anymore. You murdered them all."

"I've found new members."

"I met one. I don't like her."

"We're even stronger than we were before, and capable of doing so much more than we originally dared to dream. Think of what we might accomplish, now that we've had these years to grow wiser and gain in strength. More pacts and more power. Don't try to deny your talents or capability. You cause a stir in the aether wherever you go. And you've been extremely busy since you left."

"Not that I've enjoyed it much."

"When has that ever mattered?"

We could have gone on like that forever. The pause lengthened. Those rocks that had crushed Giles Corey but failed to break him seemed to regard us witches with contempt. Jebediah stared into the dirt and I knew what it was, and from whose grave it had come.

"Aren't you even going to ask if anyone else lived?" he asked. "About what happened after you left, who fought and who was redeemed and who died crying in the mud crawling on their shattered legs? After all this time, now that you're back, aren't you even curious? Another survived, you know, even if you don't truly care. I'll tell you anyway. Only Gawain lived."

I already knew that. Gawain had survived, protected in his unique blind and deaf muteness, but I didn't want to think about him.

I said, "They're dead because of you. Whatever you've got in mind, let it go, Jebediah. Draw Iblees from me and cease this Fetch and maybe we won't have to kill each other for another few years."

"Are you sure we have to?"

"Let's put it off a little while longer before we have to find out." The burn slash rose like an eyebrow cocked in offense. "But I swear if I have to look at you for another minute here, we'll have our death match now. So I'm asking you, please, let me go."

The lip quivered, skewing his smile even farther. "So, it is true. I'd heard whispers in the circles that you still pine and rage, and Bridgett mentioned you refused her gracious offer of flesh."

"Listen—"

"You're still angry with me for what happened to Danielle? You've actually never gotten over those adolescent urges?" He had a natural talent for making the most meaningful aspects in life sound so hideously insignificant. "You're better off really, if you approach it from an objective point of view. In time she only would have destroyed you."

Calm down, Self told me.

What?

Don't . . . don't . . . shhh . . .

"I'm willing to pay what you most want," Jebediah said. "I'll help you bring her back whole, with her entire soul, if you'll rejoin me."

"That's impossible."

"You really ought to know much better than to ever say that to me."

The venomous rage caught me low in the guts and Self growled and nearly doubled over. "All your faith and four hundred years of knowledge, your deceits within the craft and deals in the devil's circles, and you still managed to ruin the authenticity of our last sabbat because of your insecurities and inadequacies, Jebediah."

The color drained from his cheeks, making the bags under his eyes stand out farther. "You've no right to judge me," he whispered.

"You're a failure as Grandmaster, leader, and friend. Rather than lunge and parry for the remainder of our lives, let's skip the banter. We've always known it would happen this way."

"It didn't have to come to this," he said.

"Perhaps not a decade ago, before you

shoved us all into hell. Not before you killed my girl. Now it does, Jebediah."

"For you have said so."

How we enjoyed our tortures. The monks of Magee Wails Island had developed a taste for vinegar and self-flagellation with cat-o'-nine-tails. Danielle existed as the most perfect core to my soul and the greatest horror of my conscience—guilt was a salve of sorts, and one I wouldn't give up. Jebediah demeaned love like no one since the Inquisition.

I remembered how she would laugh and compliment him on his wit and character, proud of our brotherhood, so trusting in me, and me in him. Her face kept flashing in my mind—beautiful and wet as she'd once been lying on the shore of the pond after we'd made love, sediment in her eyelashes and water cresting on her naked shoulders—and spitting blood, choking in the church, and grinning a red smile.

"You're insane," he said, and I burst out laughing. So did my second self, slapping his knee, and then we looked at each other and suddenly it wasn't so funny anymore.

Jebediah tried to chew his lip but that tooth kept passing through the tear. Fiery shimmering sigils began to float and flame in the air before him, products of his madness, or only mine. He wanted to play with the dead some more. "I still need your help," he told me, "but if you need to die to become willing, then by all means, proceed."

"Sounds good to me."

So many hints and taunts and minuscule torments. He'd enslave me after death, if he could, like the rest of his soulless minions wandering the house, just another eggshell puppet and afterimage of the doomed. Jebediah's body brimmed with spells, crimson sparks now skittering along his fingernails, popping and arcing to the buttons of his vest. He stroked his goatee.

The majiks in the room soaked the back of my neck, those cursed authors returning to some trace of life through their lore. Why the hell not? We all knew one another, and what had brought us to this. He held his fist out and the occult violet flames burned up his arm the way they had that final sabbat night.

Pierre's lute began to play, the plucked strings straining for melody. Antiquity is myth, and his past was steeped in the shrouds of witchery from the hanged to the hangsman.

"I actually did need your help, you selfish son of a bitch," he said calmly, and made as if to fling the fire at me backhanded.

Self dove from behind Jebediah, grabbed his wrist, and wagged a claw under his nose. *No, no, none of that. You sent the invitation but that doesn't make you King of the Hop.*

"You never knew what to do with this companion of yours."

You talkin' to me? You talkin' to me? Self's DeNiro needed a little work. *You must be. I'm the only one here. Peck in the Crown couldn't put up with your folly any longer.*

Jebediah refused to address Self directly. "It's grown far too articulate and willful. It even has your face. Can't you see that you've given too much of yourself to it? Perhaps you're not as strong as I thought."

He hurled the flames up into Self's face, grabbed him by the throat, and heaved him high over the desk. Self flew backward across the room into the far shelves and landed atop a copy of the grimoire of Pope Honorius. His feet dipped down through the binding as it opened wide on its own and rippled like a black pool. Self grimaced and tried to get free. He bit and tore at the book, his knees drawn into the cover, sinking deeper and deeper until it had swallowed his legs and was sucking him down farther.

What have I done that you treat me with such disrespect? he asked. His Brando wasn't much better. The pages bulged as they engulfed him. He squealed, *I could use a little help*.

Jebediah shrugged off his jacket and I saw the muscles rippling on his wiry frame. I jerked back my arm and launched a Mohammeden hex straight toward the point of his chin, hoping to fry off that pretentious goatee. The tomes around us pulsed with our passions and hatred. Mesopotamian dark spells flowed from my fists and battered aside the Philistine fires and rising cones of incantations burning within him. Welsh Celtic war cries and epithets from the Zohar spilled out between those creased lips. He fused sorceries in fashions never done before, and still I sensed he was holding back.

Self attempted to find leverage by driving his claws into the binding. It ripped and bled like flesh as he was drawn deeper, his chin nearly under the pages. He said, *Uhm, hey now—*

Hold on.
Oh, that's helpful.
The strings of the lute twanged out melodies that Jebediah's raped ancestors had been forced to listen to, slower and sweeter than those Bridgett and I had danced to in the restaurant. I didn't have many defenses here in Jebediah's lair and he hammered away at my mind and soul as our wills met and spat and battled savagely.

Gawain entered from the other side of the room through a pair of sliding doors, and I felt the pressure of his presence rushing against me.

Born perfectly normal, Gawain had been brought home by his mother and immediately had his eardrums punctured, corneas seared, and tongue snipped so that it forked. He'd been raised as a feral and pure child and led into the craft. Without those senses he was unhampered by the tactile world and found realities beyond it.

Bridgett stood beside him and struck her pose once more, all those curves doing wondrous things again. Self's mother perched high on her shoulder with talons tangling in her hair. Thummim stroked the two sweeping curls away from Bridgett's mouth. Behind them stood the dwarfish corpse of the governor and another dead man painted black and white like a harlequin, sticking his tongue out and making faces. His hat and clownish costume was full of bells that jangled as he pranced closer.

Even demons know some form of love. Thummim screeched and reached for Self but the various tomes about the library glowed brightly and whispered at her proximity, snapping open, reaching for her. Forty-seven years before the birth of Christ she'd ridden the shoulder of Julius Caesar when he'd ordered the library of Alexandria razed, hoping to destroy the *Ta Biblias,* the earliest Hebrew Bible. These books would never forget, and forever be her enemies.

Jebediah hissed, "Stay back," and Bridgett lifted her chin and blew me a kiss with those exquisite pink lips. Thummim jerked toward her as if a leash had been yanked but continued to shrilly squawk and stretch out for her child.

"Sorry, lover," Bridgett said to me, as perfectly unerotic as possible. "I'll have to make you some other time."

Please! Self cried. Paragraphs and diagrams from the books scrawled over his face now, running black and red.

I was barely holding my own. I reached into the depths of Jebediah and found the silver cord tying his own vicious soul to him: rusted and sharp as razor wire it slid against my psychic reach and cut me deeply. He tried the same thing, hunting for my heart, digging and driving past the ghosts of my life. He sought all the sweet weak spots, and I slashed him worse. I held back a scream and the blood poured into my mouth reminding me of Danielle at the end, so beautiful and broken.

He laughed out the back of his throat. "Not that easy. You don't even know what to do with your hate." His soul was at ease with its fury, the cord sheathed in something I could feel but couldn't manage to cut through.

There are times you've got to just duck and run like hell.

I rushed over and punched him in the face as hard as I could and knocked him on his ass, the dirt from the grave of my love showering over him. I hefted one of Corey's rocks off his desk ready to crush Jebediah's skull but those minor blazing sigils floating in the air spun in front of my nose and erupted like mines.

No time. I whirled and plunged my arm

down into the Black Pope Honorius's grimoire just as my drowning second self faded beneath the pages, his mouth stuffed with the mad pope's curses. My mouth and nostrils were suddenly full of scraps of paper too, the script writhing and spilling upward, crawling off the papyrus. I grimaced and shrugged backward, hauling Self up, the writing holding on like nets pulled tautly across his head. Words were written across the whites of his eyes. I planted my feet and dragged him out inch by inch, Pope Honorius's ink slithering loose and finally splashing back into the volume. Self and I tumbled to the floor and lay there gasping.

Thanks, he told me.

Always my pleasure.

"We're going to resurrect our coven," Jebediah said. "I need them still, and I can't do it alone. The pacts and vows make it far too meticulous and exacting for my talents. You're the Lord Summoner, master of the art. You will help me."

Gawain, dressed in a lavender cloak, his bleached white hair and pale lost face nearly translucent in the night—my friend for a time back when I believed we could be friends—mouthed my name, that serpent's tongue slithering forth, and blindly held out his arms for me.

Behind him the harlequin tittered, and I knew I hadn't quite reached the lowest depth yet. His voice was familiar. A shiver quaked through my spine and I slowly turned to face him.

There the fool stood, lips and tongue black, unimaginable weariness written into the painted and ashen lines of his silly white dead face.

Oh God.

My father.

Chapter Four

We circled the altar beside the covine tree, where the original wiccans had respected nature and been crucified for their integrity, bleeding into its roots.

Like a dozen of those forgotten bodies twisted and knotted together, the limbs of the tree grappled in the snow, some branches gnarled and collapsed backward upon themselves, others hanging like weeping willows. The north side of the trunk had been sheared off that night by lightning, and it spawned new mutant leaves that remained green even now as the freezing wind blew.

Our covine tree stood as an ode to irony—

our kind had been hanged from it, burned upon it, nailed to it, and still it lived, and still we lived. My father muttered to himself and continually regarded me as if he retained his mind. He wedged his fingers into his ears or puffed out his cheeks as if he were the entertainment at a children's party.

Bridgett enjoyed touching the dead and moved her hands over his white face, kissing and licking his nose, trailing her fingers over his groin. In life my father would have tried to persuade her from her path, but eventually he would have been beaten down by her nature and given in. He always had.

Thummim swung from Bridgett's left breast, and Self dangled from the right, taking turns suckling the witch's teat.

"Sex majik won't work at this stage," I told her.

"In resurrecting witches? No, I'm sure, but when it's needed there's no one with as much natural talent as me."

"So you keep saying."

Piercing green eyes like sharpened jade, offset by those dark brows—her features contained even more than she knew. A whiff of that salvation and church scent came wafting by. She had taken her vows as a novitiate seriously at the time. "Think what will happen on Oimelc when we make love, Lord Summoner."

"You're not my type."

"Yes, I am. What kind of errant arcana will run wild then, as I ride you at the Feast of Lights? Did you give all your passion to your familiar, or have you simply buried it?"

He's hiding it, sweetie, Self said, kissing her breasts. *My needs are my own. Let me show you.* Thummim giggled and clapped, tickling my second self under his chin as if to say, Yeah, that's my boy.

The djinn hadn't done as fine a job on the crypts of the mausoleum as they had the House of DeLancre.

Tombs of the Knights Templar were built in an early Norman shape called dos d'ane— the tops triangular with ridge mouldings exiting from an immense stone horned skull. The head at the top is the honored point of the tomb, leading down into the vaults. Jebediah trailed his fingers across the doorway, spelling out necromantic treaties and other symbols of resurrection. The horned skull had once been a sign of mankind honoring the natural order and his place in it before becoming bastardized into the image of Satan. It dipped and opened its mouth. The door shuddered and slid back.

Eidolons, wants, and terrors seethed within. I caught pieces of visions from the last sabbat. They were so strong that it was like being struck with shrapnel. Those forces raged and knocked me backward into the tree. I could sense the murdered members of my coven flowing around me.

Elijah's hatred was as strong now as ever before, although it felt as though Griffin had forgiven me. Bridgett tittered and her familiar Thummim grinned widely, as much lust streaming into the air as anything else. Because she hadn't been a member of the original coven she couldn't feel the power of our binding with the dead. That stink of the church drifted beneath the musk of her sex.

Jebediah grunted and struggled forward against the errant thoughts and hour of death emotions that still eddied about the tombs. Gawain, the most sensitive of us, clamped his hands over his deaf ears and dropped to his knees in the snow, mouth open in a silent groan as that serpent's tongue twisted fiercely. Perhaps he was hearing the shrieks and caterwauls from that night, or maybe something altogether different.

Self dropped from Bridgett's chest and folded around my throat, licking the drops of blood off my upper lip.

How does your mother fit into all this? I asked.

Perfectly.

Tell me, damn it.

I have.

The nine murdered coveners whispered and hissed, sounding even more hideous than Arioch's voice of the endless damned.

Jebediah could barely contain his excitement, a nervous jitter in his step. "Won't it be delightful to see them all again?"

"You're insane," I said, and he burst out laughing.

We stood before the crypts of our brethren, feeling them in the air around us.

Rachel and Janus, both pregnant, she with their child and him stuffed with the yoke of Fuceas, demon earl in charge of thirty regions. Both of them lying at the feet of Danielle as she tried to carry them to safety, their bloated abdomens bursting.

The triplets Diana, Faun, and Abiathar, caring more for wine and women's roller derby than the teachings of the friars who'd raised them. At once they were geniuses at the craft but also hopelessly divided over their cause. The widening fissure between their conflicting beliefs cost them their lives as the three of them, drunk and brawling that last hour, hip-checked one another into oblivion.

Griffin, Keeper of the Salamanders, a firebug completely intoxicated by flame. He'd finally allowed his appetite to get the best of him and burned down a children's leukemia hospital before arriving late to the sabbat. He'd been the first to die, drooling flame, with my blade between his ribs. The fire had poured out of his chest while his dying angry gaze softened, both of us surrounded by the vengeful ghosts of children.

Elijah, who'd loved Danielle almost more than I had. He wanted me dead as much as he wished to face his namesake, the most holy of prophets.

And retarded giant Herod, the only real innocent, who'd known what would happen long before it did, but none of us had listened.

A slab had been set in the empty tenth vault with Danielle's name chiseled on it, as if Jebediah still waited for a time when he could recover her from a grave full of my protective charms in Calvary. I didn't need anyone else to raise Danielle. I'd had my chances before and I knew it wasn't worth the price. Like my father, she would never be the same. Too much of her soul had fled, and I didn't dare discover what remained. It might be too much like her to resist. I'd stopped her own teenage sister from digging at her majik-steeped grave, bent on revenge.

Elijah's living hatred swelled in the darkness. Jebediah shoved at the slab and it creaked aside with a hollow roll that echoed throughout the tombs. He reached into the crypt and, like a careful lover, placed his hands gently against a shadow within and drew it into the light. It was a woman's body.

With his split tongue slipping out both sides of his mouth, Gawain made a sound of caution at the back of his throat.

Jebediah's beatific smile grew only mildly more sadistic as he spun to show me his hands, moving his fingers down the cream-colored angles of flesh inch by inch, pressing against golden hair and burrowing as though digging though graveyard dirt.

"What game is this?" I hissed.

At last, after another anxious moment, he revealed the face of my lost love, Danielle.

The edges of my vision turned black, then red, and I crumpled. "Oh my Christ, you bastard."

"I got her for you."

Dani. All our nights together, the wash of the pond, and the shouts of our fathers. My life, my girl in her crypt now as beautiful as ever, somehow remaining as perfect as always. God, I never could have expected this. My broken charms lay strewn about her corpse like the petals of her prom corsage. Even with his new coven it must've taken him a thousand hours of fiddling with my safeguard spells to unearth her. But he'd been willing to do it.

"Aren't you pleased?"

My father skipped from foot to foot, clapping and chuckling as the bells on him rang. He kept going, "Woo woo, woo woo." He seemed to recall Danielle as he peered into the tomb, or perhaps he only remembered that part of his life before the paint, back when he lent me the car on Friday nights to take her to the movies. He'd died trying to save Dani as much as me. He'd been damned himself for nearly as many reasons as I'd been, and I wasn't sure which of us had proven to be the greater failure.

Now he had another role to play. Our ill-fated coven deserved a doomed mascot. Maybe he saw himself the way he was meant to be—dead in his coffin, at rest, a fool perhaps but not a harlequin. Gawain tried to calm him, both of them making gurgling noises.

Bridgett said, "She's not that pretty."

Jebediah stroked his sparse goatee, his eyes almost bleeding his obsessions without any discernment. Perhaps in heaven one sin really was just as bad as another. But not here, Jesus no.

Dry heaves backed me up to the other side of the crypts. That freezing slate felt white-hot against my neck. I staggered back to Dani, and though my hand trembled I managed to touch her arm. Her flesh was neither warm nor cold. I could barely keep from climbing up onto the slab with her. The ancient words were already on my tongue because I so desperately wanted to raise her now.

I croaked, "Let her go. Let them all go."

"That's not what you truly want."

"Jebediah—"

"I didn't actually bring you back here, you know. You simply accepted your fate as it's entwined with mine. You have the enlightenment and knowledge to aid me in our quest."

"What quest?" My father shambled along beside me, trying to stroke Dani's hair. "You don't need me," I said. "You have a new coven."

"Not quite. I've got my eye on a young necromancer who is quite powerful, but remains untested. You'll meet him eventually. Regardless, no one in this age has your skills as a summoner, not even me, and I need your help in raising one other dead man."

"Who? Who's worth all of this?"

"We're going to force Christ into returning to earth a little faster than he'd apparently like."

Self giggled and said, *Way cool!*

Insanity like dream holds its own internal reality. Besides vision one needed belief—truth, if necessary, would follow later. The thought tickled me. Jebediah DeLancre, lord of the djinn and of everyone I'd ever loved—in sheer audacity, if there was anybody capable of being father to God, it was he. Telling Jebediah that he was insane would only be repeating myself.

He said, "You know it isn't out of the question. He was a man."

"Ascended bodily to heaven."

"I think not. Study my research. There are volumes I own that you've only heard of in rumors and legend. Imagine what comprehension and insight he holds on the Sephiroth and Sephirah, on the Infernal hierarchies and the lowest circles, and God Himself."

"You don't want to do this."

"We could force our way into paradise and sit at His left hand." That tooth shone against his lip like the spear point used to stab Christ in the side. "It's why we need to raise our coven again. I need their aid from the other side, to bring Christ closer to us. They're already near. You'll need blood."

"No," I said, at last understanding what the game was, and who the players were. I moved but wasn't going to make it in time. He'd already drawn his athame from his vest pocket, and with one fluid stroke he cut Bridgett's throat.

Her eyes widened in shock but there was something else there too as she stared at Jebediah and the knife, fingers coming up to toy with the heaving flaps of slashed flesh at her throat. I suppose she'd been half expecting him to murder her the entire time.

Bridgett pirouetted and flopped over into

Gawain's arms. Blood geysered and spattered Danielle's burial dress. Thummim danced beneath the arching stream, and Self too fed on her arterial spray, gulping loudly. They hugged each other with their mouths open, mother and son sharing quality time, the power of corrupted blood flowing through us all.

"Why so unhappy?" Jebediah asked. "You would've had to kill her soon enough yourself. She had a few mannerisms that reminded me of Danielle. I'm sure you noticed as well. Odd, wasn't it? So different but with so many of the same attributes, and her ploy worked. She wasn't particularly adept despite her sensual glamour. Believe me, her sexual promises were exaggerated boasts."

My back teeth clacked together. *It was a setup, all right.*

Would you rather be dead?

"This isn't about Christ," I said. "You simply want to be with Peck in the Crown again."

Jebediah ignored me. Gawain held Bridgett and surprised me by actually weeping, his alabaster skin streaked with red. Death he understood but betrayal did not exist in his brutally honest mind. Her sex poured in a puddle surrounding him. Gawain was perhaps the most noble of our coven, or merely the least hampered by being human. He remained something that was both more and less than the rest of us: the child, the beast, and the sage evolved beyond any hint of the commonplace. His seared eyes searched for me, mouth aquiver with tears as he growled his dissatisfaction with these events unfolding. It scared the hell out of me because I knew that if this was enough to make him cry, then we were into something awful.

Jebediah scribbled symbols before Gawain's face, explaining himself. "She's not the Maiden of the new Coven. I've found someone substantially more talented."

"I can hardly wait to meet her," I said.

"You will on Oimelc, the Feast of Lights. We'll have the glory we once did. Danielle will live again on Oimelc. Whole, as she was. As you and all of us loved her."

"That's impossible."

"I've tracked and collected each portion of her soul. She can be yours, alive, the way she was meant to be, if only you'll rejoin me. Think of it. Your love in your arms, with the chance for true happiness, even a family. That's all you've been dreaming of these last ten years."

"You maniac, you've no shame at all."

He pulled back his arm and slapped me with a palm covered with Bridgett's blood, then backhanded me, and did it again. "Now summon them, damn you! That's all you've ever been good for! Call them! Do what you must!"

I did.

I summoned myself.

With my arms outstretched and hands flat against the icy tombs, the waves of energy pounded and revolved about me. My words were clear in an amalgam of antediluvian languages, both human and non. Self fell over quivering, caught up in the maelstrom. Thummim rocked him, squealing. I wondered what Christ might actually say to us face-to-face, and how jealous God would become, and whether we'd ever be forgiven.

So close, my love. Our forgotten youth, the feel of your thigh on my cheek, the way I dragged you into an abyss of my own making. If only my father had possessed a bit more foresight, or been a little stronger, maybe we all would have survived our pursuits.

I called forth friends and enemies alike. Elijah's ghost had its hands in front of my face trying to show me something that swayed before my eyes. Maybe it was his heart, maybe someone else's. His mammoth rage was red.

Jebediah had shrouded his soul within the heart of the dead coven, hiding among those he'd destroyed. I shouted, "You god-damned coward!" and snagged a silver cord in my psychic teeth. Janus and his children from Fuceas urged me on. Snapping first one, then another and another, I watched the ghosts kicking and stirring. All the while I made entreaties to Azreal to release their spirits. Jebediah hadn't expected anyone to toy with his own incantations, and he looked startled seeing me snarling in the crypts. Self realized my intent and worked at the tangled spells. *Relax, relax, I'm here*, he said. *Leave this to me. Continue, get on with it*.

I did. Griffin, Keeper of the Salamanders, had forgiven me, and helped unsnarl the souls. I cut the other lines but my coven didn't stray far, no matter how hard I shoved them off toward the afterlife. This wasn't going to work. What a waste. I locked gazes with my father and reached for him, praying that he was still in there and would remember, for a minute, our lives before the madness brought him here to his own murder.

I held out my hand and said, "Dad?"

My father bit me.

My blood dripped into the pool of Bridgett's blood on the ground. It was my will that coursed here, my resolution and no one else's. *Nice thinking*, Self said, *but are you sure you know what you're doing?*

Let's hope so.

I am. I do.

I called forward what I needed. My father guffawed and capered around the tombs. Thummim sat on his head and spun around with him. The sweet scent of maleficia and rage filled the crypt, and in the House of DeLancre I could hear the walking corpses shrieking in fear.

Far too late Jebediah cried, "Wait . . . !"

The doorway to the altar filled with shadow.

And standing before us, smiling in all his sadistic eminence once again, strumming his lute and covered in snow, and with his hatred for witches and family as tangible as the six hundred people he'd once sent to the stake, stood the perverted witch killer Pierre DeLancre.

Chapter Five

Self said, *Pierre, my man, lookin' dapper. Play us a new tune. Something with a backbeat.*

The witch-hunter had learned from the progeny that had enslaved him all these centuries. He played his lute and all the raped and slain women from the Basque danced to his melodies once more: they remained his captives as much as he was theirs. I shied from his evil, not just the depravity from which he'd climbed, but what had come along with him. Spirits crammed the crypts, so many of Jebediah's line that he sought his face in all of them. The dead governor had followed Pierre from the mansion and now swung arm in arm with my father to deranged ballads. The tombs filled stuffed to bursting with the horrors of Jebediah's family.

As Pierre approached, Jebediah whimpered, "No."

I'd have to say that the boy is seriously pissed.

"Stop the Fetch, Jebediah," I told him. "Release Danielle and my father, and I'll send Pierre on his way."

His jagged lips crawled. "And you called me a maniac."

All those wicked thoughts and feelings caged within Pierre DeLancre these hundreds of years now roiled in his burning eyes. For a face that hadn't grinned in centuries his mouth now parted in a distorted smile to show black teeth. The skin of his face snapped and ripped because it had grown so taut over time.

Only one word escaped him, with the fury and lovingly obsessive passion that had made him a legend across history. His vicious, psychotic laughter rolled crazily in the back of his throat until finally he spat. *"Witches!"*

Even as his master I shivered at that voice. Jebediah grew nearly as pale as Gawain, his scars standing out like flames. He wasn't only scared of Pierre's vengeance but also of all those demented souls of his ancestors. What confessions might they drag from him?

Those dead ancestors that Pierre De-Lancre carried on his back wheeled and flowed across the crypt and pummeled Jebediah. They'd watched him, they knew him, and they were privy to every secret and failure and fear. The House railed and roared with iniquity and cruel humor. No guilt was beyond their grasp, no hidden dread could remain concealed. Jebediah might enjoy confronting his victims, and might even delight in defying God, but his own family surrounding him now simply reminded him too much of himself.

Who's brave enough to face that?

Self curled around my throat, waiting for the action to really get going, with a witch-killer on the loose again. *C'mon, Pierre, let's clean it up once and for all!*

Jebediah handled it better than I would've thought. He held out for another few moments, the cold sweat streaming from his forehead as they approached. His muscles tensed and he wet his ragged lips with the tip of his tongue. His burn scars darkened.

"Get rid of them!" he cried. "The Fetch is off! Iblees will mark your step no longer."

"Let go of Danielle and my father."

"I can't."

"Then screw off."

"I can't! Our destinies are too snarled. Take your father with you if you like, he doesn't amuse me anymore. But Dani must stay. She's a part of us. And no matter how much you argue the fact you know I'm not lying to you."

Pierre DeLancre, killer of hundreds of witches, turned to look at me, and his eyes were crammed full of hatred. He didn't want to go anywhere. Pierre and his ladies drifted back a step and then another, unfurling as time took its natural course, and he faded to dust in the midst of all the women of the Basque he'd raped, who now stamped on his ashes and cursed me.

We could find our gods and even speak to them if they weren't too deaf or indifferent; we could hide inside our greatest joys and successes, but no matter how much time went by or how much blood ran we could never extricate ourselves from our own dead pasts.

"Betrayer," he said.

"Now that's a good one."

I backhanded him and he smacked me and I backhanded him to the floor. Despite all our power, all the deaths and dreams having already cut us to pieces, it still only came down to two men slapping the hell out of each other.

He raised his bloody face and struggled, like Christ. "Oimelc, the Feast of Lights sabbat, is in six weeks. You'll be back."

"No, I won't, Jebediah."

"We'll be waiting for you, our Master Summoner. The breath of God has already shown you the way and the truth."

"We make our own truth. That's why you're so sick." I scrawled fire before Gawain's face and said, "You can come along if you want, Gawain." He looked at me as if I were an even bigger fool than my father. Thummim waved to my second self, black tears dribbling down her coarse face, but that mouth still tilted into a knowing smile.

Jebediah leaned heavily against Danielle's tomb and spun away, dismissing me without even a gesture. "In six weeks, then."

I left the tombs and walked to the northeast of the covenstead, working through the thickets on a downhill grade past the pine

and sage as my father stumbled along behind me. I grabbed a handful of snow and
tried to wash his face, only to realize that
the black-and-white harlequin paint was
actually a mystical tattoo. It would take me
a long time to get rid of it, if I could at all.
We stared at each other and he leered and
made nipping motions.

Deep in the woods I finally ran out of
steam, dropped to my knees, and bawled
like a baby. I kept wishing my father
were here to comfort me as the fool
clicked his heels and tittered. He'd once
tried to save me, and for his failure this
was his reward. I wasn't certain if I'd be
able to steal what remained of his life, especially now in the midst of so much killing and resurrection.

He broke for the brush laughing and kept
going on farther into the forest. I ran after
him for a time and eventually allowed him
to go on alone. Perhaps he'd be more free
this way, untied from both me and Jebediah.

Snow burned with the opening light of
dawn as I fought through the heavy brush
and broke onto the path leading toward the
church.

I wouldn't be back.
I wouldn't.
Self yawned and said, *So what are we going to do in the meantime?*

Part Two

Mount of the Oath

Chapter Six

Cliffs rose sheeted in ice that glared red as the dust of Masada.

At the top of the mount stood a place of massive triumphs and torments, where blood on the rock never faded. Culled from fervor and faith, Mount Armon ascends snowcapped and glinting in the coming dusk, hard and undying as the martyr's soul. There are holes in history that can't be filled, eons occasionally still muttering, and gaps into which the restless can be drawn or pushed, straining empty-handed toward ritual and the hope of redemption.

Magee Wails is only made an island by the gorges surrounding the mount and the

Tom Piccirilli

forked river that converges into James Lake
a quarter mile below the towers of the monastery. Those who dwell there are the
damned but perhaps not the doomed. This
river has baptized ten thousand, and
drowned ten thousand more. Within memory there have been hurricane seasons
when hordes of escaping rats rode the swollen corpses downstream, as they did the
early Christians in the sewers of Rome.

The first Christian hermits lived on the
shores of the Red Sea. They soon joined
with the Therapeutae pagan ascetics and
consequently moved into upper Egypt to
avoid Roman persecution in the third century. Pachomius and Anthony Basilica
were the first to be called monks, and their
lessons are written in the bronze door
friezes and bas-reliefs that surround the
monastery's chapel.

Even from the river's far bank the gleam-
ing honey-colored stone and wood of the
service buildings can be seen like flashing
threads of silver, grouped around a cloister
south of the church.

Silhouetted against the moon, the steeples, turrets, and angled spires of the abbey
appeared to be basilisks appealing to
heaven in the falling snow. Empty branches

of ash-gray trees partially obscured the large peaked roofs. Sheep were still kept, but more for the symbolism of lambs and shepherd than for any practical need. Bleats poured down the precipice like hymns gone astray.

The mount is a city unto itself where few have been turned away but even fewer saved. Penitents came from a hundred nations carrying beliefs that sporadically conflicted with one another. Though the shadow of Babel fell on them there were hardly any strangulations or midnight stabbings anymore, and only a few dozen nuns had become pregnant in the last five centuries.

I'd spent six months here a decade ago recovering from the last sabbat. Once I'd thought the monks and nuns too sequestered from the rest of the world, but I'd learned their distance gave them resolve that could only be weakened by contact with society. This was the final sanctuary where the despondent came seeking refuge from their sorrow and distress, from their knife-wielding ex-husbands, their greasy uncles' paws. Anguish that sometimes still drove them to jump a thousand feet down onto the crags and into the waters until the ice was thick with suicides.

I was sick again.

I came starving out of the mountain passes. Every breath rattled deep in my chest and felt like serrated blades sawing at my lungs and catching in my ribs. My phlegm had turned a dark gray and became speckled with blood two days ago. I kept blacking out on my feet and waking up lost in the snowbound forest. Phantoms held at bay for years were invited in to taunt me again. I couldn't protect myself. I talked out loud and saw my father dancing behind bushes. Maybe he was there or maybe I only dreamed it. The bells on his little hat chimed as he peered at me with that hideous harlequin smile, but at least he led me toward the water.

My vision grew too bright around the edges. I awoke on my hands and knees at the shore of James Lake, staring into a wavering reflection I didn't quite recognize. Danielle's mournful cries echoed against the precipices of the cliffs and the jagged ledges of my mind. My second self nuzzled at my neck, with my erratic pulse driving against his fangs.

You handed your heart away, he said.
Take it back.

She deserves it.

They won't even bury you next to her.

Sweat streamed off my face. Self licked
salt, the witch's bane, from my brow and
then spat it aside like drawn-off venom.
Black motes of energy flickered against my
forehead, spelling out my sins. Ancient
words from the Suleimans bubbled over,
and I lost control of incantations. Hexes
went haywire and the frost boiled beneath my feet until the earth dried and
cracked, and the smoldering brush with-
ered around me.

Self said, *Hey, watch it!* Lower-caste demons bounced around confusedly and
gagged in the smoke, mewling questions
and threats, begging for a lick of flesh, their
tongues unfurling from their eyes. A few
bowed and begged my forgiveness; I could
only guess how they'd influenced my life, or
what they'd done so that I should be merciful. Sometimes it got like that.

Dit Moi Etienne, who'd answered one of
my earliest invocations, buzzed and
worked its mandibles into the dirt, as if
hoping to hold on to the world through the
storm it knew to be coming. Self took my

111

hands and forced my digits into the proper positioning—interlaced, with the tips of index fingers together in a this-is-the-steeple fashion, thumbs pointed over my heart—and growled words to send the imps squeaking back up the boulders. I wondered why he didn't just tear them to pieces, and whether it was a matter of pity.

They croaked, scrabbled, and cursed him. Talons scratched on the stones, throwing sparks into the river. My familiar waved and blew kisses, carnage in his sharp smile. *Sorry, boys, you wouldn't like it here much anyway. No cable.* He turned to me and threw his arms up in a patronly manner, cocking a grin. *They're big on the Playboy channel.* Beneath the mask of poise, however, there was fear. He sliced open his palms with his claws, and I understood that death hung by closely. He kept spitting over his shoulder, hoping to ward off Azreal, angel of death, who can't be dissuaded. I knew because I'd tried and failed before.

I fell face forward into the snow and gasped, my breath hitching painfully in the center of my chest, and soon found myself weeping bitterly. The ice steamed where I touched it, my fists burning with other charms of my making. He did his best to minister, but the virus had gotten too far inside my head. Too much had already gotten out. I turned and turned again, hearing my mother singing behind me. Danielle gestured and whispered. My father waved and stuck his tongue out at me.

I tried to keep the pleading out of my voice, that whine working at the back of my throat, but it came through anyway like a scream. *Don't let me die yet.*

Self grinned because he always grinned, full of life and the happiness I'd always wanted. *You won't die.*

No?

You can never die.

Where's the ferry?

Less than five miles. I can help. He glanced toward the towers, and the muscles in his throat rippled. Fiery glyphs burned as he spoke, fumes of the blood scent wafting from his mouth. I knew what he was thinking. He could rape, maul, and kill one of the nuns in a half hour, and feed me the strength. *Let me help, damn you.*

Stay away.

His tongue snaked over his lips at the thought of the red pouring onto the white, a pair of broken hands clasped in prayer, legs spread wide, the agonized look on the faces of the crucifixes as the various Christs watched. His joy was overwhelming, and I bit down my nausea. *Stop it!*

You'll thank me later, you know.

I wanted to live, and the most clever part of his temptations was that I could always shift the burden of my conscience onto his shoulders. He couldn't offer to do anything for me that I hadn't already thought of on my own. That bait dangled, the trap set.

More hours of insanity passed. Through Self's eyes I saw myself twitching and lurching in violent shrieking fits. My howls swung up the gorge, and perhaps a keen-eared sister heard me, nodding without satisfaction that someone was growing closer to God through penance. It was always possible. They were used to the lamenting, and the timbre of contrition: they flagellated themselves nightly, and most of them still didn't know anything about pain.

Danielle came to me again as she always did, arms outstretched, skin tan and glistening from the pond where we'd made our love so many times—at once beautiful and betrayed, with a mouthful of blood. She stood superimposed in my vision, dark and glittering, and no matter where I looked or how I thrashed my head she remained directly in front of my face. The world could move but we never would.

Whatever happens to me, don't let Jebediah finish raising her, I told him. *She deserved her freedom and peace. Promise me.*

What?

I charge you with that duty.

He hopped around angrily with his lips writhing. *You can't do that!* Maybe not, but he sounded unsure.

I can.

You can't!

Jebediah would try to raise her again on the next major sabbat, the Feast of Lights, Oimelc, on February 2, now barely three weeks away, and his new gathering would stoke his madness even further than mine had before. He wouldn't be able to do it without me, and I had to resist. They'd help in his scheme to draw the powers of my eradicated coven. His living witches would attempt to raise Christ before it was God's will. They would be destroyed as we were. Or worse, they wouldn't be.

A ferry with an intricately designed pulley system had been built to allow travelers to tow themselves across the river to Magee Wails island. It was the inaugural trial, the first lesson. To enter the mount one had a duty to autonomy—crossing the waters with conviction and purpose if not wisdom. The surface of James Lake had frozen in spots and ice floes floated past. Hands would be torn on the thick hemp rope, and more sweat and blood shed into the mouth of the river.

I collapsed hauling the ferry halfway across the lake. I shivered uncontrollably and stomach cramps like spear thrusts kept me curled with my knees to my chin. Some kind of an unbinding had started that needed to finish.

Memories twisted with fantasies and we were all there on the ten-by-ten raft as I dry-heaved through the remainder of the night. The cold rope occasionally cracked me across the face like the whips the monks used to beat in their own humanity. I didn't want to die. My eyelashes became fat with ice crystals. For a moment I thought I saw Self praying.

I went blind from time to time and woke up in the dawn with Self sitting hunched over my brow licking my tongue. My shirt and coat were torn open, and my running blood hissed where it hit the freezing wood. The stink of seared flesh filled my nostrils as his foul breath eased down my throat, sweet and horrible. He'd jabbed two of his burning claws through my chest bone to massage my heart and slowly resuscitate me.

Archangel Azreal hovered at my feet with a hopeful expectation, waiting. I weakly fluttered my fingers at him. Self caught stray wing feathers and crushed them to powder, turned to the seraph, and said, *Get lost, you prick*.

I sank back into sleep.

That squeal of the pulley dragged at my consciousness, the slow rhythmic motion of the ferry jarring me awake as it was pulled back to the mainland shore. Self had rebuttoned my shirt wrong and my collar tugged at my neck. I turned over and lifted my head.

Three of them stood on the bank staring at me: the mother who was white as a fish belly with two blots of windburn on her cheeks, the pregnant teenage girl, and the boy with dozens of suffering dead faces leering like balloons tied around his neck. The mother watched me closely, and her ire crawled through her eyeballs and launched at me while her children pulled on the rope together.

"Don't touch him, Catherine," the woman

barked. Her voice was too moist and her tongue slid around in her mouth like a sea snake. "Leave him there." Her nose had been broken several times so that it tilted in every direction. Her lips had been sewn back together not quite properly aligned, and the matted gray scar tissue around her eyes had trenches of crows'-feet. Whoever had beaten her must've busted his fist on her chin. That jaw set the entire bottom of her face at a strange and ugly angle, showing nothing but antipathy.

"We can't just leave him," Catherine said. It took the kids time to haul me back to shore, and they were out of breath when they carefully climbed aboard the ferry. I tried to sit up but couldn't make it all the way.

At least eight months pregnant, Catherine had to squat down before she knelt to put her ear to my chest. A low growl worked at the back of Self's throat, and he twisted tightly against my throat, sniffing, glancing side to side. My brain ached for Danielle, and whenever Catherine hung against me in a certain fashion, trying to help me to my feet, Danielle's face stood out above her own features.

"Eddie, help me with him," she said. The

boy moved onto the ferry, but he was smart and didn't come near. The wind jerked at those ghastly heads that hovered above him. "He's broiling with fever, Mom."

"He won't die," the woman insisted, wanting me to die. Shadows swarmed around her hips, all of them bearing her own face. "We could roll him in the river and he wouldn't stay down. Take your knife to him, go ahead, just try to cut his throat."

"Don't talk like that."

"The devil takes care of its own. Me, you, your brother, we might be killed here, but look at him, out in this freezing weather all night with nothing but a summer jacket, and he's still alive. Of course he'll live, and so will that freak you're carrying. Put rocks in his pockets. Kick him over."

I'm taking this bitch out, Self said.

Inside my nightmares my coven ringed around me again, standing with us on the raft. Herod dipped close and I saw his giant, cheerful, stupid face. Danielle spun in front of my eyes, afraid, and drifted off as if running.

Self listened hard for a moment and snarled, *He's back.*

What?

He's come back.

Who?

My skull throbbed as if Self were using his fangs to dig out infection, or jab it in. I rested my face against Cathy's belly and heard malignant chortling rumble deep within. I knew that laugh, and the sound of it sobered me immensely, slashing through my daze like a billhook. It was Elijah.

Self crooned, wanting to peel the scar tissue from around the woman's eyes and drop it down his throat.

Cathy said, "Lie back, don't try to get up. We'll get you there." She began to unbutton her own coat and place it over me, but I shook her off and nearly made it to my feet. I tried again and managed to stand.

"Who are you people?" I asked.

Shivering, she blinked twice, her notably thick eyelashes swiping the air. "I'm Catherine Kinnion. This is my brother, Eddie. And my mother, Janice. Don't listen to anything she says." She couldn't help looking around at the heads circling her brother and dangling in the air, sensing they were there. She had no idea about what she was carrying. "We need to get to the monastery too."

"Take your hands off him, Cathy," her

mother said. "Before his stench gets on you."

"Stop talking like that, Mother."

"You won't die," I told them. "None of you will die here."

Kinnion. The name didn't mean anything to me, but somehow she was carrying Elijah, who still wanted me dead. He was now closer to Danielle than I was. I wondered if this would upset Jebediah's plans. As a reincarnate. Elijah might care more about raising himself than raising Christ, and it might take years for him to grow into his skills once more. He whispered threats in my ear as he sought to be reborn, and I could almost see his fingers scratching on the other side of her uterine wall, greedy to get at me, hoping to steal my love.

"My uncle is the abbot," Cathy said.

"John."

"Yes."

Self pressed his nose to her navel, the milk in her breasts already curdled, and said to Elijah beneath the skin, *Hey, buddy, two words for you and your resurrection: diaper rash*.

There are no coincidences. Even in the icy breeze the air stirred with the hint of ozone, the drawing of threads of power.

The poltergeists perched on Eddie's head and slicked back his hair. He and his mother worked well together, heaving on the rope hand over hand like sailors hoisting sail, hauling us across. The boy said nothing, and I couldn't get a bead on him. He didn't seem troubled, upset, or flustered, and smiled pleasantly when I caught his eye. Cathy rested beside me, patting my knee.

Kill her now before Elijah takes over completely. My second self's jaws worked in a frenzy, the stink of nuns and monks everywhere. *That's what they're going to want you to do.*

Why should the order care about him? What does Abbot John have to do with this?

He shuddered with impatience and sneered at me, looking so much like my father that I reached out and put my palm to the side of his face. *Abbot John will call for blood. Kill her.*

And prove the woman right? We're getting out alive.

No, we're all dead and always have been.

Chapter Seven

The Opus Dei choir chants of the daily services drifted in the wind: part song, part plea. The brothers often lapsed into several esoteric languages preserving their rites and secrets. When we'd almost reached the shores of Mount Armon, I fell to my knees once more. With an air of indecision Self snapped his claws together, wondering if he should carve into my heart again, and knowing I'd made another big mistake.

On the mount sacred oaths were taken to a new degree, and even the most careless promises held power. Swearing to keep someone alive might result in my own sacrifice. Elijah continued his attack from the warmth of the womb, griping about love just like everyone else. The ferry creaked along. Soon the rope became heavily smudged with blood from their wind-cracked hands. We struck shore and the sheep began to shriek.

Blond hair draped into my mouth, and Cathy gave me a look of flawless pity. She wouldn't be able to lift me alone. Eddie helped, and after a time the mother too. I limped off the ferry, struggling up the curving stone trail forged and smoothed into the side of the mount.

Above us we could see the church and sheltered arcade cloister, the sacristy and refectory, and the snow-covered transverse tunnels leading from building to building. I glanced back and watched the ferry being drawn once more to the far side, and I wondered if my father the harlequin would be joining us tonight.

It took over an hour to make it to the top of the mount, and by then Cathy was near fainting. We held on to each other for support, wheezing in harmony. Self had chewed and snipped free most of Eddie's knotted specters, but the poltergeists continued to float around us like scared children, staring wide-eyed and wandering in confusion. Self was feeling crowded and bit a few in the ass to get them moving, taking out chunks of memory and heartache, but they only smudged themselves harder against the kid. They shuddered in Eddie's armpits and hid in his ears, moaning.

We stood before the outer ward wall of the monastery, staring at the doors with bronze friezes showing images from Revelation and the lost books of the Bible. Scenes from Wars of the Lord, Thomas the Gnostic, and the Book of Enoch reached out, with displays of loss and atonement swirling in the metal.

A copy of the Book of Enoch had been in Jebediah's library. It was a tome devoted to the human and not the hallowed that had been discovered in Abyssinia in 1773, a region of Sheol and place of the wicked. It recounted the story of the two hundred insolent angels who swore a blasphemous pledge against God. They consented to the fall in order to take human wives, and then descended upon Armon, the Mount of the Oath.

A young monk with a shaved head stood there watching, the purple welts across his face bright in the sunlight from where he'd accidentally struck himself while scourging his shoulders.

Janice wrenched my arm forward, dumped me into his chest, and said, "Take him, you idiot." She knew her way around the abbey, and led her children straight to the priory. Her shadow fell heavily across her son, and the signs I read showed Eddie on the floor, disemboweled. The puzzled monk didn't know whether to go after her or to help me up first. He started walking me toward their small infirmary but I resisted and aimed us for the sacristy. Self gave a deep sigh and snuggled against my chest. He loved churches.

Follow them, I said.

No, that bitch gives me the creeps.

I leaned on the stone and felt the waves of the ages rumbling against my back. Inhuman antiquity walked here, filled with human frailties and failures.

It hadn't been easy mending on Magee Wails, and would be even more difficult this time.

The monk had smashed out a couple of his front teeth so he might be able to form ancient cruel words not meant for a man's mouth.

"Take me to Brother Aaron," I told him. "Or Uriel."

We walked the white-stone pathways along the cloister gardens, past the basilica residential buildings. Other priests and acolytes descended the crude pine steps of the scriptorium and stared. Despite being surrounded by the lush expanse of forests and rivers they still carried the desert with them. They'd taken the most severe and unyielding tenets of the Cistercians, Trappists, and Benedictines, and used the harshest doctrines to try to garner harmonious results. They were kidding themselves, and some of them even knew it. Hollow faced and grim in the purpose and rigors of the soul, the heat of their beliefs beat into them, searing as deeply as the sun off the sands of Persia.

Aaron DeLancre stormed down the passageway with his sword drawn, and both Self and I growled. The veil of evil draped over his entire family. They could follow the bloodline with ten generations of doctors or accountants and they'd still smell like the Inquisition. Uriel also appeared from the scriptorium and did his best not to mouth any curses. They both looked exactly like their brother Jebediah, with the same broad features and sorrowful mantle of those born of witch killers. They even kept beards, but only so they could yank out handfuls of facial hair, the way the Roman guards had done to Christ.

Aaron held his sword just as men in the 1950s used to hold their cigarettes, with an easy charisma and a touch of vanity. "We know why you're here."

Of course they knew, but I had a duty to swear it aloud. "I'm going to have to kill your brother." The chills began to wrack me again and the darkness rolled across my mind.

"God help us," Uriel said.

Self guffawed at that, showing off every incisor, and slowly took some of my blood.

I ranted for the next two days while the fever worked through me. Aaron and Uriel stood guard over my bed, muttering charms, with their blades pointed to the west and the east. In the hilt of his sword Aaron kept his familiar, Lowly Grillot Holt, who played cards with Self and was only a slightly better cheater. Uriel's silent familiar, known only as Nip, proved to be as somber and melancholy as his master, and did little more than sit hunched on the windowsill peering out over the frozen forest.

Occasionally Aaron pricked my thumbs to see what glyphs my blood would spatter on the floor. He and Uriel interpreted the signs differently, but neither of them saw anything good. By the time I awoke on the third day and the fever had cleared, my blood staining the tiles had dried to a rusty powder that Lowly Grillot Holt sniffed and gagged on.

In the night, echoes of whips brought the rats squealing out of their dank corners. Prayers and chants merged with sobs of lonely despair and the scuffling of sackcloth covers. There was some trouble with Self running through the nunnery. He stalked among them while they were at prayers, sniffing the incense and shuddering with pleasure. The scent of souls was thick in the air, cloying but heady.

In the past few days two men had already leaped to their deaths into the river, where the crush of ice floes made the corpses look as if they were dueling with one another far below. Age rumbled in the dirt. There was laughter, giddy and saccharine, underscoring thousand-year-old hymns, and the goats gnawed steadfastly on weeds grown in the cracks between blocks of immovable history.

My promise held more meaning than it should have, and I had angered antiquity. Metal moved as if alive. Scenes in the bronze friezes changed almost hourly, always shifting the way the word of God is forever altering under interpretation. Beautiful penitents scarred themselves with coarse clothing strung with bone slivers and barbs.

Some of them didn't know whether to set the fire or stand against the stake. Perhaps both. And below it all the thrum of conscience flowed from the heart of time.

I sat with Nip on the windowsill, staring out over the abbey and the sisters and monks, the travelers and the lost, smelling the freshly baked bread and opened wine. He gave a six-hundred-year-old sigh that blew tufts of gray fur clear of his quivering nose, and resettled his meaty pink paws on his knees. I could see why he and Uriel got along so well, with this acceptability of silence and uncountable sorrows.

I had to check on the Kinnions.

I could feel the protective power of my own rash promise running out. There wasn't much time left.

In the early evening, when the sun began to settle and the members of the choir hit the same repulsive pitches they reached during their scourges, Fane hobbled in and came to test himself against me.

At that very second signals and symbols abounded. Dogs howled deep in the valley and the temperature dropped ten degrees until my breath billowed and hung in the air. The ice floes drew away with a tremendous groaning. The corpses flopped against each other like exhausted opponents and finally rolled into the lake.

Self drowsed fitfully and uncurled slowly, his eyelids hooded as he blinked at me. I could feel the wheel drawing on, events loosening and becoming fluid again. My oath couldn't stop the motion of the mount, and once more we began our slide toward a ruthless fulfillment.

When I'd last been in the monastery, with my Dani's blood still ingrained in the skin of my hands and neck, Fane had lurked at vespers with his own chronicles written in his eyes. A failed seminary student, Fane eventually became manager of a shoe store and spent most of his time gambling away his paychecks until his wife walked out and moved in with her lesbian lover. He'd been dead for twelve minutes on the operating table after his Harley back-ended a flatbed trailer and he went wheeling through the plate-glass window of a pizza parlor, killing three people and crippling a cheerleader.

Now he went to great trouble in order to properly portray the enigmatic, all-knowing monk furtively prowling the corridors. He wore a severely pointed Vandyke so that his beard angled and split into two sharpened prongs, the way he must've thought the druids kept theirs. He always wore his black habit, scapular, tunic, and cowl together, subverting the identity of the man he'd once been. There was a corrupt scent on him I recognized but couldn't quite place. He'd recently bathed in heavy oils and had made splints from freshly cut pine. He broke his own legs two or three times a year hoping for a touch of redemption or admiration for his self-pitying martyrdom.

Fane was perhaps the one man in the monastery who had not come to appreciate the totality of the dead past. He believed that experiences could be sliced and sorted, with certain events taken as truth while others were cast aside. It's how the Gnostics had piecemealed the Bible, choosing alternate versions of chapters and abandoning others, which led to such confusion and absurdity over the millennia. He didn't have the conviction of a soldier of God, and didn't have the arrogance a vessel of hell required. He had no familiar because no familiar would have him. Like most of us he'd lost and found God—and his soul—several times over already.

He carried several of Eddie's poltergeists in his hands. He reeled them across his fingers like twine and threw them at my chest. Nip turned to glare at us for a moment, then went back to sighing at the waters below. Self mumbled at me and dropped his head to my shoulder, snuggling.

Fane staggered closer. The poltergeists clung and swirled around us, and for the first time I noticed they were all women, and they were fading.

He said, "They're free to leave and die elsewhere but they don't. They trust you, even though you're not worthy to be here."

"Fane, you're a shoe salesman from Cincinnati."

In the last few years he'd devoted a good deal of time and a portion of his essence to his studies. I could feel the straining effort of his will in the structure of his spells. He had a separate well he was drawing from, a depth outside himself—perhaps love, perhaps perversion. Even the poltergeists sensed it, and wavered wildly.

"Do you wish to confess and do penance?" he asked.

"More than anything, but you won't hear it."

When he put his mind to it and recited his evoking prayers in a whispered litany, his face receded into shadows beneath his cowl and it looked as if his clothes emptied and drifted aloft. He drew strength from the weakness of his legs. His voice sounded as if it came from somewhere high near the ceiling, bearing down, with the hushed noises of shattering glass and his out-of-control Harley resonating distantly. A nice effect, and probably a lot of fun at a birthday party for a six-year-old. Mental fibers of his angry unconsciousness pressed outward.

"Is there a particular reason you're starting this?" I asked.

"Of course there is."

At least he was honest. "Feel like letting me in on it?"

"You've done damage."

"I could say the same about you." The

noises of the men dying and the cheerleader getting her legs crushed dwindled.

"You've much to account for."

Not only had he been training, but in the past few years he'd picked up a superiority complex somewhere. "Try to hide that judgmental tone a little better, Fane, or someone might think you were beginning to grow smug."

Down the hallways several doors shut at once and the sheep bleated in perfect harmony with the wind. Just another part of the production—pitiful in a way, but also empowering. Even so, I sensed a certain sincerity in him that didn't fit with the attitude he was throwing. Perhaps I was merely jumping to conclusions.

"Why are the Kinnions supposed to die?" I asked.

Without any face he answered, "So another might live."

"What do you people care about Elijah?"

"I care as much as you."

"No," I said. "You don't."

"The prophet Elijah ascended bodily to heaven—"

"Jesus, Fane, I don't need a Bible studies refresher from the likes of you."

"—the only man to do so besides Christ."

"The prophet Elijah didn't die, he ascended alive."

"And according to Jewish faith he will return to usher in the coming of the true messiah."

I squinted at him. "You people don't really believe this is the prophet Elijah returned, do you?"

"Some might," he said, his voice above, behind, and in front of me. "And they might do anything to protect him."

Or kill him, I thought.

There wasn't any anger here. No righteous wrath or petty intolerance. His grin shone through the blankness like that of the Cheshire Cat. He thought he was being honest and proud, but I could see his fear as the air warmed again. "Abbot John would like to speak to you in his chambers."

Fane eased away limping back down the hallway, smiling almost giddily to himself. He was, somehow, a man full of hope.

"Wake the beast," he said. "You're going to need it."

The stink on him was bad milk.

Chapter Eight

Unlike Uriel and Aaron DeLancre, who'd always been destined for Magee Wails, Abbot John had been born into the typical world and hurled against the mount by his own crimes.

He gave the impression of being almost as wide as he was tall, a solid block of mortal mortar who'd once enjoyed twisting the heads off dogs, raping geriatric women in their nursing home beds, and tracking families relocated by the Witness Protection agency. He'd suffered from visions and garnered a taste for the carotid. When he met my father his hallucinations ended, and in one overwhelming surge Abbot John's sanity engulfed him. Perhaps it was actually my dad's own finite rationality that had been given up, since a short time later he gave in to the rush of his madness.

The years hadn't been kind and neither had Abbot John's atonement. He hanged himself daily and the rope burns had been raw and wet for over a decade now. The graceless angles of his face folded in on themselves as if he couldn't swallow enough of the man he'd once been.

His bald head shone in the candlelight. He'd shaved off his eyebrows and plucked out each of his eyelashes. It made him look foolish, which was the whole purpose. His hands clenched and unclenched, and the veins in his wrists squirmed like centipedes. He still had the haunted appearance of a man who knew that no matter how much good he did in his life it would never equal the amount of harm he'd caused. His eyes were still clear and merciful, but when he smiled I knew his course wouldn't be swayed. He trusted me but that wasn't nearly enough. If he had to, he'd crush my skull in his fist. If he didn't kill himself first.

After all of his hangings he had hardly any voice anymore. It trickled out between his lips in a guttural whisper, like the hiss of water on a heated tablet of granite. "You've made a significant oath here."

"Yes."

"That was foolish in this place."

"Not as foolish as your believing that Cathy's child is the true prophet Elijah."

"You don't know that it's not."

"I do know, but you won't believe me."

I could tell he was eager for the rope. "You've made a heinous error that's endangered us all," he wheezed. "You have no concept of what wheels you've allowed to turn."

Or stopped from turning. "Okay, so tell me."

His fists opened again and the candlelight flickered across his palms, looking like the running blood of elderly women. "Janice is my sister." His chest heaved as he fought to control himself and all that was inside himself. "Catherine, my niece."

He couldn't say any more. His words caught in his damaged throat, his fresh wounds oozing across his scapular. I realized that as abbot of Armon he felt equally responsible for my oath as he did for any other unanswered plea or ill-kept promise on Magee Wails island. Events had already spiraled out of his minimal control. He stroked his upper lip as if wanting the mustache he'd once worn when gathering dogs from the pound.

He whispered a word I knew well.

The rage didn't need to build, it erupted alive and throbbing while my second self snored daintily with his eyes open. I breathed through my teeth. "What the hell's gotten into you people?"

He repeated himself. "Sacrifice." Even with his gasping I knew he threw a little something extra in how he said it, as if making the word his own. Melting wax dripped loudly and candle flames wavered in the draft. He blinked his lashless eyes at me. "Jebediah may be strong enough to succeed."

"No," I said. "He isn't. He won't."

"Even you don't sound very certain."

"I am."

"Perhaps you shouldn't be." Swirls of blurred moonlight made their way across the room. "I've seen the faces of the two hundred seraphim who consented to the fall, the 'sons of God, who saw the daughters of man and that they were fair.' The angels Sanyasa, Armers, Ramuel—"

"And Saneveel, Batraal, yes, I know their

names. Why is everyone giving me Bible lessons today?"

"They descended upon Armon, Mount of the Oath, and became men no more contemptible or noble than any of us. Imagine them giving up all of paradise for what was to be found on earth. Imagine how far they'd go to get what they wanted."

"And what did they want?" I asked.

"Affirmation."

I slumped farther down in my seat and tried not to sigh. "I've got a feeling that you don't know the first goddamn thing that you're talking about."

"Sacrifice is purity. I do know that."

"Are you speaking of redemption or murder? You think you can find atonement by killing children?"

"You've a narrow view of sacrifice."

"No, I don't, John."

My lost love Danielle had been an offering of many kinds to many forces. To my ardor. To the sins of my father. To the obsession of Elijah, and the egomania of Jebediah. To the virtue of her own soul. When she should have left my side at the covine tree and run for her life she'd instead chosen to say behind. In the moment of her death her integrity had been hacked to bits in the dying light of church fires, and each of us had stolen as many pieces of her as we could.

Arcane energy leaked from my eyes and mouth and drifted around the room. Hexes formed under my tongue and I kept sucking them back down. Abbot John drew back and his shining head reflected flame.

I said, "I know about loss."

"My apologies."

"If the angels wanted humanity, then they had to take everything that went along with that decision. They should have learned as much from Cain as from any other man. One of the earliest lessons of the world is that sometimes God doesn't *accept* our sacrifices."

As a man who hanged himself every day, the thought terrified him. "We . . . we are all only instruments and follow the natural course of His will."

He only heard what he wanted to hear. "Your recitations and metaphors have been puerile for twenty centuries, John, and this is a place of clarity. I made my oath succinctly, the least you can do is talk to me without such banal platitudes."

He nodded once, and his face went blank like a knight's visor suddenly lowering. "It's only partly metaphor, the rest is up to you. I had a vision. She is to die here."

"You don't have visions anymore."

"I've dreamed a great deal lately." He frowned, not wanting to share something. "Some about you. Some about Archangel Michael."

"I don't care about them."

If he had a voice he'd be yelling, but his resolve could only eke out of him in a diminutive whine. "Cathy is to die. She carries Elijah. Jebediah has sent him to herald the resurrection of the messiah before—"

"I know. It's my problem, you can't hold her responsible. I'll take care of it."

The coarse chuckle from his strained voice sounded like a handful of gravel being tossed across the room. "Your vanity is boundless."

"It's not conceit to know your enemy as well as I know mine." He wasn't afraid of the will of Jebediah. He'd taken in two descendants of Pierre DeLancre, and spent his life in a stone fortress reinforced by age and consecration. "What are you really afraid of?" I asked. "What stalks the mount?" He started to choke as if the rope were already tightening around his throat. "Tell me."

"What is here hides on its own accord,"

he whispered. "Among us now and forever. You already know that."

Self continued to slumber and I didn't know why. He never slept and even now just sort of drowsed with his eyes open. It made me nervous and my sweat dripped onto his forehead and slid into the corners of his mouth. He murmured in a language I'd never heard him speak before, and he kicked out occasionally as if running from me in his nightmares. Perhaps he was already preparing for the worst.

"You're starting to sound like my father, John," I said. It was the most awful insult I could offer.

Abbot John, looking so pink and foolish, bowed his head before the weight of the irrevocable epochs of Armon. I knew he'd go to the noose early tonight, and without any prayers he'd hang himself until he came within sight of alluring Azreal's outstretched hand.

The boy Eddie lay vivisected, his chest cavity opened wide.

The flesh had been peeled back in layers and pinned to the bed with thick needles engraved with the holy names of God.

All his major organs had been carefully

removed and set aside in ancient pottery, each vessel of terra-cotta inscribed with Sumerian, Persian, and Babylonian phrases. His rib cage had been sawed in half and set aside upon the Seal of Solomon flawlessly drawn across the glistening black tile.

Liver, heart, lungs, and stomach sack sat on display—healthy despite being extracted. The peristalsis of his intestinal tract kept pumping clean and potently. Eddie's eyes were open too.

The monks couldn't have done this alone. Not without service, provision, and *affirmation*. They hadn't become so advanced in the medical applications of necromancy to complete a ceremony of this magnitude—doing this to the boy, raising his soul before it had time to leave this plane, and keeping his life force in stasis.

Uriel kneeled in the Kinnions' room, chanting quietly before a small chantry platform of idolatry. He worked well with dolls. Porcelain figurines and wooden statuettes of saints immediately turned away and crossed themselves as I entered. Snow piled up outside on the sloping roofs, and burning paw prints of familiars, demons, and djinn formed circles around the colonnades. Shadows of furtive figures surged like children in between the columns.

Aaron stood near the door, keeping watch, his sword lashed across his back. Lowly Grillot Holt kept shuffling cards and practicing his three-card monte. Nip sat in the darkest corner of the room, facing the wall, sobbing against stone.

Self snapped fully awake with a start, kicking and yelping. He didn't recognize me for a moment and drew his claws back to rake off my lips. Then his nostrils quivered and he sniffed, smiled, and stretched until his vertebrae crackled.

What's the matter with you? I asked.

Me? Nothing. What's wrong with you?

Aaron approached. His grimace described his honest confusion and helplessness. He hefted his sword and cradled it, hands fluttering because he knew there were seldom foes that could be cut. The monastery thrummed around us; the skeletons of two hundred angels who had become men were now only dust in the breeze. We breathed them in and could taste their insurrection.

"This was simple poltergeist activity," I told him. "Most of the eidolons were snipped away before we even arrived on the mount. You should've been able to cure the boy with a mild charm. What happened?"

"You should know more than us. You deal with the dead. He fell into a coma and soon died. We resuscitated him and thought it best to eviscerate."

"You did this, Aaron?"

"No, I haven't the ability. Uriel and some of the other friars and mendicant worked in tandem, as directed by Abbot John."

"Can they actually cure him this way?"

"Abbott John believes so."

"I don't."

He shook his head. "Neither do I." Finding nothing else to cut, he worked the blade across his thumb, finding resolve in his own angry flesh. The red droplets ran down his forearm but he couldn't bleed out his frustration that easily. "All that's keeping the boy alive is your oath." He gestured toward the beds. "We need your help. The mother won't let us near."

Janice sat beside Eddie holding his hand, her eyes much more dead than his. Her cheeks were drained of so much color that I could see each of the burst capillaries in her face. She stared at the row of jars and seemed to be focusing on his heart, beating and still alive. She looked as close to the line of lunacy than I'd ever seen someone stand and—perhaps—not yet cross.

Eddie said, "It's not so bad, Mom."

Now that I saw her again, in my right mind, I could make out more clearly the fiber of her sins and guilt. Her life stood as open and empty as her son's body. I knew whose knuckles fit the indentations of matted scar tissue, who'd fathered her children, and who'd murdered her dogs.

Cathy sat up in bed and stared at me over her swollen belly. She said, "I was getting worried, but you've recovered."

"Yes." The honeysuckle caught in my throat but I managed to ask, "How are you feeling?"

Self cackled savagely.

"They're . . . they're taking good care of us." Her face twisted out of focus and became clouded, as if seen underwater. With a ripple it suddenly shifted into a guise containing too many emotions at once. She was terrified and in shock. Her smile seemed soldered to her face. She almost couldn't make her mouth muscles move enough to say, "Can you help my brother Eddie?"

"Yes."

"Will you?"

"Yes, I promise."

She reached over and stroked my face, and for a moment the contact felt electrical and made my cheeks flush. I could see the curse in her genetic alphabet, the corrupt arrangement of her doubly recessive genes. Children of incestuous relationships are occasionally polydactyl. The small nub of the extra finger they'd removed from her at birth scraped along my jawline. She glanced down at her belly and rubbed it with slow circular motions, the same way Elijah had begged Danielle to do to him.

Cathy said, "My baby hates you."

"I know."

Janice snapped her chin up, as if taking the first breath of her life. "Of course it does." She waved me over and said, "Come here, I need to talk to you." The murder in her voice was as distinct as the palpitation of her son's heart in the jar. "Hold my boy's hand."

I swallowed thickly. "He's going to be fine."

She carried her own ghosts. Other versions of herself, mostly without the scar tissue. The same but also different women, some of them smiling and waving to me, some of them not making love to her own

149

brother John. All her unborn lives flung themselves flapping over her shoulders like flayed hides or old clothes no longer worn. The fever had made me stupid. The poltergeists that had been strung across Eddie, all of them women, were other forms of Janice, clinging to her son in order to protect him. I never should have cut them free.

Self sat on the headboard and crooned some hushed Sinatra tunes to the boy, swaying as if he were performing in front of thousands of teenage girls. Eddie beamed.

What's going on here? I asked. He didn't want to stop singing, and I had to wait until he finished the chorus of "Strangers in the Night."

You tell me. You made the promise.

Help me to keep it.

You can't keep it. You never could.

He crept across to Catherine's bed and sniffed at her womb, then swept her hair from her eyes. I knew he could make one quick incision and give her a cesarean section if it became essential, or if he felt the need to steal the baby.

Elijah's animosity, for once, slumbered too. Self dropped off the sheets and put a hand on Nip's shoulder and whispered in his ear. Nip nodded once and continued to weep. Lowly Grillot Holt approached them for a game of five-card draw and Self screamed, *Stay out of my face, you little cheating bastard!*

Janice stared at me until my incompetence must've spilled across her feet. Her ghosts trusted me even if she didn't, and they urged me forward to comfort her. I waited until both Cathy and Eddie were asleep, listening to Uriel's murmurs and Self's wonderfully moving singing voice.

Janice Kinnion said, "If you try to touch either of them, I'll kill you."

"I won't touch your children."

"They sent you here. He sent you here . . . my brother."

"No, he didn't."

"They want her dead. Are you gonna tell me you don't know that?"

"No."

"I came here for help and they've gutted my son and now they're trying to kill my daughter and what's inside her. And they keep pretending this is a home of God."

Sadly, it was, and that proved to be the ugliest irony of all. "It's been a home to many things," I said. I sounded vague and misleading and wanted to nail my tongue to the roof of my mouth.

She chose not to argue. "Can they do what they say? Can they make him whole again?"

That was two different questions. "I don't know. They can probably heal his body."

"What goes along with the rest of that?"

"I'm not sure."

"Come on, come on, out with it already!"

Reason had its place here, but not as an eternal truth. Discord arose minute to minute, and belief broke its own back from the way men bent it to their own devices. There was always a price to be paid: for every midnight caress or kiss or hastily scrawled poem of infatuation, for each promise made and each disregarded. Greater affirmations had to be found at any cost.

The wars of the Lord could not end in stalemate. Sacrifice was not purity, but it meant more than chicken's blood. There were those who would slay the lamb as sacrifice to God, and there were shepherds who would protect the lamb for either God or themselves or for no discernible reason.

These walls were going to come down. The quandary of the mount made the rock itself lament.

"Something here wants your kids," I said.

"Why?"

"I don't know."

She whispered at herself, sounding so much like her brother. "I need to get them out."

"It's too late to run."

"Then I'll fight."

"Yes."

"If you get in my way I'll kill you."

The snow was on fire. Uriel's plastic saints glared and skipped along the chantry. I left the room and Self slid alongside me with a pair of aces under his tongue.

At the far end of the hallway, the empty cowl of Fane peered back for a time before straying out of sight.

Chapter Nine

My mother came to me in the night, knowing I was weak. She sang to me the way she sang before the crucifixes cracked in my father's fists, back when the priests still came over for lemonade. I could feel the texture of her presence like the downy blankets of my childhood, when the apples fell in the corner of our backyard. I lay there and couldn't keep from panting like a sick dog. Self ran around the hemp mattress on all fours, yawping and sharpening his claws against one another.

At the foot of the bed, a nun smiled timidly at me. She held up the hem of her robes, showing off the luscious angle of her legs. The great whore burned in her gaze, the harlot gilded her lips. She pulled off her headpiece and let it drop behind her. She winked and winked again, eyelid fluttering while the tic moved across each muscle of her face contorting her features. Tears hung off her chin. She swept forward, trying to throw her hips into it, giving it some Mae West, but she'd been in the nunnery for so long that she couldn't quite remember how to even try to seduce.

Her hair had been shorn to a Joan of Arc pageboy bob, which somehow only accentuated her feminine qualities. She giggled to herself, the glow of moonlight catching her knees. Trails of blood dripped down her inner thighs and speckled the floor. She began to sway and the spatters widened into ugly omens. Those earthy sniggers became even more revolting, and finally they deepened until she didn't sound like a woman anymore. She glanced down to read the warnings in her own blood, and the struggle inside her became more clearly defined.

Self had finally managed to win some money off Lowly Grillot Holt, and he held up a dollar bill. *Take it off, baby!*

She drew her habit over her head and threw it swirling behind her. I saw that she had the marks of Jezebel on her, the dog bites and the painted face.

Ooh la la!

Self sauntered forward, quivering and clapping. His arousal drove a white-hot spike into my forehead, so that all my barricaded cravings and desires released at once into my veins. The blood lust had always fueled and intoxicated him, but never like this. My pulse ripped at my neck like pincers. I snorted loud as a horse.

Nun ninnies! Mas garbanzos!

Stop it!

I held on to the back of my second self's head with one hand, and clasped the other over his mouth so he wouldn't lick away the portents. I tried to read them but the slate gulped down the blood. The nun crooked her finger at him and offered up her small, pointed breasts. I tightened my grip.

If you're not going to take advantage of this situation, then I am!

What's happening to you? I asked.

I ain't no damn priest!

Other figures flailed on the floor, wagging and heaving like a carpet of snakes as they fondled and masturbated. More hermits, sisters, and penitents drawn into the dream. Elijah's living hatred bulged in the room. The glamour had been cut loose. It latched on to them in their passive state of *apatheia* even while they sought *gnosis*, the knowledge of God. Anything could be corrupted.

I spelled out fiery exorcistic rites in the air, but they did nothing except light the room further. Hands and faces were darkly bruised and red with welts, their backs and asses running from the cat-o'-nine-tails. Self broke free and dove away. I arched on the bed with every muscle inflamed. They giggled wildly, and so did he.

And so did I.

Orgy time!

Thoughts of Caligula and the senators' wives packed my head, and the stench from the vomitoriums made me gag. I flung myself forward and tackled Self hard, pinned him down, and bit deeply into his shoulder.

I took some of my blood back and his enraged screams brought me awake a little more. The women coiled around my ankles and knees, but they didn't want me or anything like me.

You bit me, you sick bastard!

Stop your crying.

What're you, crazy?

I had less control over him and he had

much less control over himself. I held his eyelids wide open and looked inside him. *What's gotten into you?*

Me? he mewled. *What's gotten into you?*

What the hell are you doing?

Hey, they're begging for it, you friggin' prude! Shit, I need stitches!

Quit it!

I dressed quickly, grabbed him by the arm, and tugged him from the room while he screeched. I fought not to scream when he sank his fangs into my wrist. My blood splashed against the black hallway walls as I marched outside into the gusting snow. I made it to the outer wall and yanked back the huge wooden plank of the main gate doors, and stared at the bronze bas-relief friezes while they roiled and surged like molten metal.

It showed two new faces among the frothing others.

Both of them blinked and calmly watched me sweat in the blizzard.

"Gawain is coming," I said. "And he's with my father."

Chapter Ten

I waited for them all night in the storm.

Moonlight ignited the swirling swells and billows of snow. There was no other watch. At some point, one of the acolytes came out and tried to place several thick woolen blankets over my shoulders. When he touched me the embers of arcana blew back into his face and he cried out in surprise as his teeth glimmered blue and orange. I stood freezing in the rising steam with the snowfall melting as soon as it hit me, the wind alive with flaming sigils. It was getting rough out. Self glowered at me but said nothing. My oath had taken its toll on him as well. The more I held my ground the farther we split apart. The wheels of the world turned out of sync, grinding and squealing and waiting for the grease of sacrifice.

I'm sorry, I said, but he didn't answer.

Uriel plodded through the knee-deep snow to stand beside me, staring down the cliffs uncertainly. In all the time I'd known him he'd said only a handful of words to me. He remained stoic as stone, immovable perhaps, but never unfeeling. Even his brother didn't know his capabilities or the extent of his convictions. He wore dangling crosses, some inverted, others not. The ebb and flow of his hidden inclinations brushed against me.

Eventually he picked up the blankets and wrapped himself in them. Occasionally the living idols would clamber over his tunic, gaze around, and squeak to him. Nip was nowhere in sight, but his tears flowed from Uriel's brow as if he were sweltering. The plastic saints started playing peekaboo. Uriel's prayers were of a kind I'd never heard before. He spat wards into the wind but they froze in midair.

After another hour, as the blizzard worsened, Uriel gestured to me and said, "Don't peer into that darkness too closely." He spoke little enough, but managed to really say even less. He turned, fought his way through the snow, and plunged back inside the abbey.

Time became tangible and smeared all around me. The weight of the past came down again, bloated and crushing. I no longer heard my mother singing. Instead my father's giggles reigned over me. Maybe that was the way it was supposed to be right from the beginning. The steam dissipated, and so did the majiks. My fingers grew numb. I fell over and shaped a snow angel for myself. I nodded off, slumped against the gates. The friezes rolled under my cheek. I slept for a time and only awoke when my father's frigid bronze lips kissed me.

I couldn't see much of anything besides the thrashing snow and revolving hexes. I thought I heard jingling and I spun around, listening intently for the sounds of my dad's humiliation. There was nothing but my heavy breath in the battering wind. Self frowned and pointed high. I shielded my eyes and looked up.

The possessed nun who'd tried to seduce me had climbed out my room window to stand shaking on the ledge. She'd gotten dressed again, and the folds of her habit fluttered and rippled like a spreading black stain. Thick ice rimed the precipice. Hands groped for her ankles. She inched along the ledge, reaching back to steady herself against the rampart, but continued on. Other people sprouted from the window trying to reach her. They began whipping themselves right there, invoking God and other deaf creatures. The bride of Christ crouched and waited, denouncing herself before the vast chasm and crashing floes below.

She managed to smile though, and plucked at the snowflakes in front of her face. I thought I could understand why she might do that. Perhaps because the flakes, at least, were so close and solid in an otherwise ethereal place. Her arms came up as if she could hang on to the air, and simply step out onto the falling snow and drift back down to earth. She leaped and floated, or maybe flew for a moment, buoyant in the howling jet stream. Maybe the mount didn't want to let her go yet. Perhaps it would pull her back inside. She hovered there for another instant and dropped into white silence.

Is this my fault?
Ask yourself. My ass is cold.

Gales ripped across the courtyard. I got lost along the outer curtain. I stumbled towards the monks' Chapter House and found the access tunnel to the cloisters but the doors were frozen shut. I wandered and lost my bearings. I fell asleep again for a few minutes, until more jingling bells roused me and I came awake half buried and shivering violently. I wondered if they'd abandoned me or if I'd deserted them instead. Self was gone.

The moon had set but there wasn't any dawn. I felt utterly alone and thought of Christ in the garden of Gethsemane. While he awaited the kiss of Judas and the arrival of the Roman soldiers, Christ could have called on twelve legions of angels, but he went to his fate alone. What guts.

I followed the jangling toward the inner curtain and back into the monastery. Two sets of wet footprints led a trail to the west wing.

I'd waited all night and had still missed the return of my father.

That awful stink of burning tallow wafted on the draft. Smoke formed new shapes of damnation. Ash on the walls spelled out the names of my high school graduating class, rows of those who hadn't become students of hell. Supplicants and monks lined the corridors, giddy and anxious. Assertions were being made.

Priests murmured their masses as I stalked past. The tinkling bells withdrew farther into the distance. I heard a baby crying, and I started sprinting.

They'd put Gawain and my father in the highest tower, near the principal hall of the church. I took the stairs three at a time and barreled over acolytes. The hushed crowd huddled in the narrow stairwell and fought to get a glimpse of what was happening. I threw elbows and shoved past everyone, hoping to hold in my rage and failing as usual. Incantations boiled from my mouth and eyes, and my touch set fire to their cowls.

Abbot John tried to slam the tower door in my face and I howled my hexes into his chest. He blew over backward into Aaron's arms, who looked at me deciding whether to draw his sword. We could go this route if they wanted. My teeth wriggled with the taste of coagulating spells. Aaron kept his hand on the hilt of his sword but didn't attack.

Self said, *You're late*.

My father skipped from foot to foot, giving raspberries and chuckling. Just another dead man harlequin sticking his tongue out and making faces. The bells chimed on his hat and clown costume. My hair was thick with ice crystals, and when I turned aside my curls rang together in harmony with my father's jangling. I had a flash of déjà vu. This had never happened before but it would happen again.

Gawain held the infant in his arms, and I knew he could hear Elijah's whispers. He stroked the baby's head as if trying to calm Elijah's fury—or perhaps he merely wavered before he squeezed the soft spot of the child's skull.

While I'd waited all night, another clown in the storm, comparing myself to Christ on his way to the crucifixion, Cathy had given birth in the house of her enemies.

Gawain had survived the destruction of our original coven, and the permutation of the one that followed. I thought he could endure almost anything. Protected in his blind and deaf muteness, eardrums punctured by his own parents, his long white hair fell across his face as he stared at me with his seared corneas. His forked serpent's tongue slithered between his lips. I

167

wondered what it was that he found in me.

He was still dressed in a lavender cloak, his pale lost face nearly translucent in the torchlight. I tried hard not to run. He remained something more and less than the rest of us, a holy man in an unholy place. The younger monks pressed their foreheads to Gawain's feet and listened intently to his silence, hoping for revelation. I'd done it myself back when I'd first met him.

Gawain made no motion or gesture toward me or anyone. He sat holding the baby and anticipated nothing I understood. He was eternally patient within the retreat of his own mind. I couldn't be sure if he'd come to the mount in order to aid me against Jebediah, or if he actually wanted to help resurrect Christ.

Abbot John's lethal hands kept twitching, capable of twisting all our heads off, but he was impotent before the beauty and promise of Gawain's unreadable face.

John's chest still poured wisps of smoke from my hexes. I glared at him and said, "You'd take a newborn from its mother?"

"Haven't you criticized enough?" The petulance in his throaty whisper almost brought an anxious bark of laughter from me.

"Did you have to kill Janice to take the child?"

"No." He bore his blame well, and hardly looked humbled for having been his sister's lover. "Cathy is sleeping comfortably. After midwifing the birth, Janice collapsed. She hadn't slept in four days."

"That's because she knew you were coming for the infant. And her children." He didn't even bother to nod. "Eddie's condition?"

"The same."

I looked at the baby but couldn't tell its sex. "Is it a boy or a girl?"

"A girl."

"I won't let you have her." I wanted to murder somebody, and the killing strokes swirled around in my palms, growing more and more concentrated. "Are you the father? Did you sleep with your daughter as well as your sister?"

Those hands came together in a bash of bone, clasped in prayer. "I should kill you."

"Is that one of your affirmations, John?"

In some obscure sense he might have believed Cathy and Eddie to be unclean, the products of the profane union of himself and Janice. If he wanted to completely wipe out the man he'd been, he might also want to destroy all that man had given birth to.

But I didn't quite believe it. I might have considered him capable of murdering his own flesh if only I wasn't so certain that he'd find suicide a more courageous act of martyrdom. He probably wouldn't have throttled his own kids—but the baby?

"Revoke your oath," he said.

"No."

"You'll be destroyed, and we'll all die with you."

"Nobody else is going to die."

"You fool."

I might have too much ego, or not enough, but a promise of protection was still valid. I struck the rock behind me and could sense its sickness. "No one else leaps from the buttresses. Nobody else gives in to misery. Not even you, John. You're staying off the rope tonight."

The thought of not torturing himself made him frantic. His hairless pink face became even more ridiculous, and he looked like a piglet trying to escape a butcher.

Gawain offered the child to me and I held the infant girl. I felt the newborn soul entwined with Elijah's despondency. There was nothing of the true prophet Elijah here, but Jebediah's greatest strength was in forcing the verse of scripture to fit his intent. Maybe I was supposed to be the one to sacrifice her upon the altar of my fears.

"She's beautiful," I said.

Give me the kid, Self told me.

What?

Give her here.

No.

I'll keep her safe.

Where?

Trust me.

Are you back? I asked.

Are you?

I handed him the baby and he took her gently, careful of her fragile neck, and hopped away down the tower stairs. Monks and nuns fell over themselves. Abbot John dove and missed, and Aaron's panic crowded his eyes. They ran out to give chase.

If the mount hadn't been so set in its course and manner its spires and roofs might have come thundering down now, if only to state its case. The charge in the air grew until tiny pinwheels of ball lightning sparked in the rafters. My father tumbled across the room.

"Leave me," I said, and I was astonished

when all the penitents and priests left without an argument or fight.

My oath wouldn't affect Gawain, and whatever evil stalked these corridors could not drive my dead father any more insane.

"Why are you here, Gawain?"

Only he and I remained of Jebediah's first coven, but Gawain carried the others with him in some fashion, even now. He sat and stared into me, and never so much as mouthed my name.

My father grinned through his painted black lips. His leer was something set loose from a bottomless terrible dream. I floundered against his chest and held on to him as tightly as I could, waiting for his arms to encircle me, but they never did.

He kept giggling and dancing, and we swung around the room like that for a while, until I was left in a heap and couldn't catch my breath for all the sour tears coursing down my face. I cried for him with my fists in the air just as I'd done when kneeling at his grave, whimpering, "Dad . . . oh, Dad . . ."

Chapter Eleven

Cathy and Janice slept fitfully, with their hands snatching out to each other across the space between their beds. The bloody sheets had been hung aside to dry for later use, along with the stored afterbirth, which would add potency to any spell. Janice's scars took on another hue. All the ghosts of herself sat on the mattress, cuddling and patting her thighs and listening to the deep regular breathing and frequent angry snorts.

The empty robes of Fane pressed a wet cloth to Cathy's forehead. The floating cowl turned to me. Slowly his face reconciled and filled in angle by angle. He stroked and washed her brow and neck, and spoke quietly in her ear. She smiled warmly in her sleep.

Just as his features had been scribbled in, so was the truth that Fane was the father of her child.

Eddie's bed was empty, though the pins remained stuck through the blankets. His organs were still intact in the clay jars, but the jars had been rearranged. His lungs worked their steady rhythm like a bellows.

"Is my daughter safe?" Fane asked.

"Yes."

"Where is she?"

"I don't know."

He nodded, and oddly enough added, "I trust you."

"Apparently you do. Why?"

"You're the only man I've ever met who truly has nothing left to lose, and absolutely nothing to ever gain." He pulled no parlor tricks, but his voice still sounded as if it came from everywhere around me. "I pity you."

"Knock off that crap. Where did they take Eddie?"

"He vanished right before Catherine went into labor."

"When this is over you should take her and go back to selling shoes."

"Perhaps I will. As soon as Elijah is expunged and I get my daughter back." He kissed Cathy's lips, and for a moment my jealousy grew as bright as Elijah's. Fane wiped her face again and said, "I used to think being a shoe salesman was hell. No wonder God killed me."

The smell of curdled milk made me want to sneeze. I left Fane pressing his mouth to Cathy's chin while Janice's ghosts glanced down at her. They saw her one poor seedy life being led despite their potential and expectations, and it revolted them. Her ghosts looked angry enough to kill her.

They pleaded and followed me down the passages, plaintive and clutching. I tried to get them to show me where Eddie had gone, or been taken, but the tragedies of their unlived lives suddenly became too much. Their teeth fell out and their gray roots kept showing through, and their husbands preejaculated and their hysterectomies left them vacant and bitter, and the welfare checks kept getting stolen out of their jimmied mailboxes.

The torchlight dispersed them. I tried more and more doors. Penitents kept their flagellation down to a minimum tonight. They chewed leather and their attempts at atonement were halfhearted at best. When the storm broke I knew that at least half of them would go back to the common world. Out there they'd be normal again. They'd screw around on their spouses and lie in confession. They'd get creative on their 1040s and forget to rewind their tape rentals, and they'd cut each other off in traffic and buy shoes from Fane that didn't fit.

Where are you? I called when I came to the chapel.

Self carried the jar with Eddie's heart in it. He and Eddie stood holding hands before the door.

What are you doing here? I asked.

Self remained silent, panting. The flaps of Eddie's chest had been shut, and he wore a soggy shirt. He said, "I want to go to the place."

"Which place, Eddie?"

"The one of forgetting."

I worked my arm into Self's mouth and slashed myself against his fangs. I fed him blood hoping to sever the link between him and whatever else haunted Armon. His Adam's apple bopped as he sucked, and he

176

soon began to burn and flood with our rage again.

Oh, my head.

You've been in contact with it.

Me? With what?

You tell me.

No, you tell me.

Where's the baby?

Safe.

Where are the others? Where's Aaron? And John?

There are no others. None who count.

He sniffed the jar and his mouth watered. I'd given him a taste, and his appetite grew as he watched the beating heart, thinking of the juice and raw flavor. The force of his own desire seemed to startle him, and he wavered a step and held the jar away from his face. It surprised the hell out of me. He handed Eddie's heart back to the boy, who held the pottery close. I felt something in my second self that I'd never felt before, and the icy sweat prickled my hair.

He'd almost felt guilty.

I asked, *What's the place of forgetting?*

Where did you hear that?

You think you can stop answering me with questions?

Can you?

Yes, I said.

L'oubliette, Mon Capitaine.

An oubliette was a miniature dungeon reached through a trapdoor that was so small only one person could be in it at a time, hunched over.

Do they even have one here?

A room of torture. Of course they do. For purging if not for adversaries. They have everything else.

It was also called a murder hole.

I said, *Show me.*

We entered the chapel. Gawain and my father were already inside. As we passed the metal stoup that held the holy water I nearly dabbed and crossed myself with it. Some habits died hard and others didn't die at all. We continued into the vaulted aisles, the arches of ashlar, and the sheltered arcade, knowing that beneath us were the cloister tombs.

The single cell of the dungeon sat nestled behind the altar, as if at any moment the priest might call someone up front and send him to that prison. The trapdoor screeched open like a terrified man. My father said, "Woo woo."

Eddie walked forward and started to climb down into the hole. Gawain put out his hand and gently stopped him, and for a second I thought he might hug the boy.

I could barely squeeze myself down into the hole.

The depth of darkness cut through me as easily and quickly as I moved through it. Self shut the trapdoor. A whole ocean of antiquity existed in every whitecapped second. There are moments of distinction when the soul stands to one side and takes full measure. The substance of the forgotten place thickened into a veil sliding over me, encompassing my corpse, a pall over my coffin.

I walked and kept walking, the levels of shadow before me, inside of me, and the endless reams behind my eyes. My father's breath seemed to heat the back of my neck. I tried to grasp my mother's songs but she was too far away, even here and now. My lost love Danielle shifted in my arms, just as she had in the pew when she'd died whispering her devotion. I could deal with the dead but only when I raised them and they didn't raise themselves. All the flaming words of my past didn't light an inch of the way. The gloom went beyond remoteness, another manifestation of doubt and regret. Like all my remorse it was never-ending, as deep and limitless as the dark where all my own failures lurked. I could go no farther.

Get me out of here.

I hadn't moved an inch. There was no place to move. The trapdoor opened.

My second self said, *Well, that was a stupid-ass waste of time. What did you forget in that place?*

Not a thing.

I was stiff and sore, but I finally knew why Gawain was here.

My father put his whole head into the stoup and blew bubbles in the holy water. It reminded me of when he taught me to swim in our backyard pool, and our dogs paddled beside him and his skin was bronzed by the sun. No amount of blessed water could wash the harlequin stains from his face.

Self thought it looked kind of fun. He clambered up the stoup and tried to do it too, but my father hogged the bowl. They giggled and splashed each other. The tiny bells tinkled until my brain rang with them.

I said, *Are you sure the baby's safe?*

Pop's a pretty fun guy! Not like he used to be.

Sometimes the despair came in too low

and fast. It slid under my guard to skewer me so deeply that I didn't know if I was dead or alive anymore. A moan started to ease up my throat but I managed to swallow it in time. My body bucked as if making a stab for a life that no longer—and might never have—existed. My legs went wobbly and then the surge of grief crested and passed.

The girl?

As safe as she can be, he said.

Gawain, as ever, stood patient and relaxed, free from the turmoil of dull sentience. His parents had prepared him from birth for excursions like these. They'd trained him by driving him out of his mind. They'd punctured his eardrums, put out his eyes, and sliced his tongue apart. By detaching him from himself they'd loosed him from the sensual world and left him to explore that enormity beyond the common touch. He lived in that darkness, disassociated from the rest of us.

A part of me had always been intensely envious of him. He remained the paragon in repose. He was blessed because no blessing would ever matter to him.

He gazed at me with those blank eyes, awaiting my resolve.

"All right, Gawain. You lead, I'll follow."

I pried the jar with Eddie's heart in it from the boy's arms and hid it in the vestibule. I set seven charms with seven locks and seven wards around the pottery. I wasn't going to make it easy for the mount to take this particular pound of flesh.

I opened the oubliette. Gawain stepped inside it easily, without bending or ducking. He slipped into the blackness of the dungeon box and faded until I couldn't see the back of his white hair anymore. I pulled my father's dripping face from the stoup and urged him toward the murder hole. He got down on his hands and knees and stuck his head into the trap. He made funny noises and did something he could never have done in life—he laughed at himself. Self snickered and prodded my Dad in the ass with a claw, and my father shot forward and fell inside. Self held his nose and jumped into the hole as if he were snorkeling in the Bahamas. I heard one of them go "Wheeeeeeeeeee!"

I took Eddie's hand and led him down into the forgotten place.

We were instantly consumed, as if the earth had heaved the mount on top of us.

This time I could feel Armon's assent. It

was like slipping through regions draped with cobwebs. I could feel the return of my own oath's affirmations. Maybe John wasn't that far off. Gawain's robes flapped against my belly exactly as they had when we'd stood around the covene tree. Even then he had no self-doubt or fractures of fear or buried half-stifled desires. Before the wedge of his purity the black curtain flinched aside, parted for him, and let us pass.

Dad chortled in the shadows. In a space not large enough for even one broken man we walked for miles. Self said, *Damn, my feet hurt!* I could hear him and my father tickling each other and tittering in turns. I kept a firm grip on Eddie's wrist and prayed that when this was all over they could make him whole once more.

He whispered, "I forget. I keep forgetting."

Let it be true, I thought. Forget everything, even in your dreams and your most awful nightmares, cleave yourself from your visit here. Do what the rest of us can't.

Chapter Twelve

Mount Armon welcomed us into the belly of its granite keep, where the crags trickled shreds of a hopeless heaven.

Hearth fires burned and stoked altars lit our way. Millennia thinned. My pledge didn't matter here and my back straightened with relief. Promises dried up and flaked off like dead skin.

Two hundred angels who willfully turned away from God had given up divinity in order to put on the shackles of mortality. On this spot they had sworn their testimony before shedding eternity and taking their wives.

Gawain's lavender robes held the firelight

and cast a purple glow against the rock. Water lapped in the distance, and the air turned much colder. We came to Jakin and Boas—the names of the two pillars originally erected in Solomon's Temple. They were supposed to be black and white, symbolizing good and evil, but both were so dirty with grime that it was impossible to tell which was which.

My father crept forward and waved a friendly greeting. Dust flew upward as an immense weight shifted. The stone grumbled and the ground swayed.

So, this was their sired legacy.

I beheld the Heir of the Mount, the offspring of Armon.

It lived upon a heap of ash and bone.

The mammoth mutant, a human-Seraph hybrid-child called a Nephilim, laid on its back rubbing its colossal feet together. It drooled down its massive silken neck. More unborn than born, without umbilicus or navel or fully formed digits, its murky eyes never settled anywhere too long and they fathomed nothing. It had no genitalia. Not only would it be sterile, but even an imitation of the act of procreation would have been intolerable to the universe.

That mouth had been opened in a perpetual silent cry for centuries. The hybrid seemed carved from shale and marble. The skin was even paler than my father's white-face. It had needs but didn't know them.

A grotto yawned open beside it. Currents of the twin rivers dragged corpses in from the bottom of James Lake, depositing bodies here where the Nephilim could dip in a hand and sup on the suicides. Heir of Armon swallowed their despondency and licked out the marrow.

In one fashion the gargantuan Nephilim resembled Gawain—separate, unique, removed, and altogether abstract. It stared blindly at him, and he stared blindly back.

Uriel's idolatry ran around my legs and he stepped free from the dark to stand proudly in front of the hearth fires. Nip sat curled, hiding his face in shame and vainly attempting to stifle his sobs.

"Glory of God be unto you," Uriel said.

"Ohboy."

Is there any myth that isn't real? I asked.

No.

Abbot John had been more right in his tenets than I'd given him credit for, and also more mistaken than he'd ever accept. Maybe the two hundred fallen angels had become men no uglier or noble than any other, but their progeny had devolved into parasites sponging off the penance of others. Those angels who'd torn off their own wings had given up too much in becoming men, and yet they hadn't gained enough to make the cost worthwhile for the rest of us.

Mankind found immortality in the thread of their blood.

Armers, Ramuel, Sanyasa, Saneveel, Bataal, and all the others—from their own ashes—must have found only remorse in the irony of their woeful living child.

It had the reverence of rock.

The Nephilim had no soul.

"I don't want to kill you," Uriel said.

"Why not?" I asked, genuinely curious.

"Where is Catherine's child?"

"Hidden," I told him.

"You can't contain the holy prophet of God."

"Uriel, I'm telling you, the reincarnate is not the prophet Elijah."

He didn't believe me. He could not distinguish between piety and fixation. For that, at least, I couldn't completely blame him. The prophet Elijah had taunted the four hundred and fifty priests of Baal into a battle of burnt offerings they could not win. When they finally admitted defeat the prophet Elijah personally beheaded them all in the name of Yahweh.

My former coven brother had dreamed of doing the same. The wrath that had been loosed from Cathy's womb would once again become the man who tried to steal my love and castrate me in the moonlight. He would be a pawn that Jebediah would use as the harbinger of a hell to come.

Uriel had no rage, but his deranged passion added up to the same. He thrust his spells into my face, They were filled more with devotion than aggression, majiks of arrogant sincerity rather than applied arcana. My fists burned black with my hexes, and I swiped aside his ridiculous sanctity and watched it skitter and pop against the walls. His plastic saints started chewing on my ankles.

My father, always the fool even when he wasn't a clown, wanted to entertain and play with the offspring of the mount. The Nephilim, sensing his damnation, reached down and plucked my dad up in one of its monolithic hands. My father gave a strange painful cry that was still tinged with his laughter.

Uriel found strength in his dedication to stone and the stone's love for him. I grimaced and tried to put an end to this encounter by letting my angry instincts take over, but the bedrock of his faith scattered my spells.

To hell with it. I brought a roundhouse left all the way up from my knees and aimed for his jaw. Nip let out another groan and flung himself away. Uriel merely frowned at me, disappointed and appalled, and dropped back into shadow. I wheeled through the gloom and ran to save my father.

If the hybrid found flavor in damnation, then my dad would be a cuisine for discriminating tastes. He didn't thrash or cry out as the mutant offspring lifted him in its tremendous fist. I dug in and rushed across the banks of bones, arcana discharging from my eyes and mouth, but the Nephilim completely ignored me.

Nip blundered into Self and Eddie, who both went over backward and lay sprawled on the cave floor.

I heard the unmistakable sound of tearing flesh and turned.

Oh, you—

Hey now . . .

You maniac!

Hey now, you wanted her to be safe.

Two buttons on Eddie's shirt had popped open and his flayed flesh had flopped aside to reveal the pink infant with her thick brown head of hair. Self had nestled the sleeping child within Eddie's emptied chest cavity.

Fane's daughter began to slide free as if being born a second time within a few hours, her tiny lips quivering as she screwed up her face. Covered with blood and mucus, her matted hair stood up in rusty clumps. Eddie's heart might have burst if he'd still had one, as the utter horror hammered him. The kid's eyes bulged out so far I thought he might have a seizure. I hoped he'd faint but he merely watched the grisliness of his own violated body.

Fumes of Elijah's madness packed the width of the cavern. I hesitated, listening to my dad's laughter as the Nephilim tousled him closer to its gritty, rigid mouth. I was torn between moving and watching Fane's daughter slip like a snake from the boy's hollow chest and slap down into the sand at his feet. I started back for Uriel.

But my own damnation must've been appetizing enough, and before I got ten feet the Nephilim rolled aside atop the crushed bone and ash and scooped me up like the hand of God. Its hungers, like all of ours, incited its mindless actions. I was hefted twenty feet in the air and shrieked as it squeezed me tightly in its giant fist.

I could barely breath and couldn't think clearly enough to provide a proper incantation. Flames spit back against my throat as I dug trenches in its reeflike bulk with my burning hands. Its oily fluids geysered in thin streams before its wounds closed. The Nephilim appeared content to raise us high up in the cavern and sniff at us, the scent of my family's destruction whisking like smoke.

Smiling hideously, Self's eyes rolled up in his head as the first wave of Seraph blood stench washed across him. Ropes of saliva lashed his fangs. His ragged laughter sounded like chips of obsidian rubbing together. In the same manner as Eddie, he seemed to fall in and out of trance. Elijah's envy, insecurity, and mistrust, like poison, splashed onto my second self.

"Now!" Uriel screamed. "Kill the baby!"

Me? Self said.

"Do it now! You too are a servant of the Lord! You cannot deny your responsibility. Slay the flesh and release the prophet!"

Self wanted to do it, he was always eager

for innocence. We gritted our fangs. We bit our tongue. His ugly thoughts pealed in my brain and I pressed my own hexes over my ears while the hybrid's flinty tongue jutted against my chest. Self went down to one knee, snarling, and managed to growl, *Boy, do you have a case.*

Uriel turned.

Aaron disengaged from the darkness, having followed the path Gawain had cleared. He moved out from the shadows with his back wet from a recent flogging, determination in his scowl.

He rushed past the hearth fires until he faced his own brother and said, "So this is where you come to pray? To that abomination?"

"What do you think has guided our hand these last twenty years?"

Aaron didn't have much to argue with, and he hung his hands weakly. "No, not this, not like this." The amends he'd made hadn't been enough, and he tore out gouts of his beard in some useless display of contrition. "And all the wasted lives? All our pain went to feeding this creature?"

"Don't be so self-important."

"How could you, Uriel? How could you allow us to continue in this manner?"

"What else would you have us do with our lives, Aaron? Here is proof that our devotion is acknowledged."

Aaron's torn back spilled blood until it pooled at his feet. "Acknowledged by this?"

"The prophet Elijah's soul returned to earth to herald Christ's second coming. We are only the instruments of God."

"Uriel," I shouted when I could take in enough air, "you're being used by Jebediah. Even Nip knows it."

Aaron couldn't truly bring himself to fight. He never drew his sword. Together they had planned to battle their brother Jebediah when the time came, and now instead he found himself alone once more, staring into the face of his hated DeLancre heritage.

They clasped hands as though wishing each other well on a long voyage, and their grips continued to tighten until their fingernails splintered and the witchery oozed under their chins. Uriel's icons and tiny saints ran around in a frenzy, shaking their plastic fists. Aaron had no resolve in confronting this sort of betrayal. Not only had he been deceived by his brother, but also by his own faith. He buckled and bent forward, and Uriel reached with his free hand to slowly tug the sword from where it was strapped to his brother's back.

The grave sound of metal slipping from the sheath made even the hybrid look over. Fate unfolded and Aaron knew it as plainly as anyone. His last seconds were nothing but humiliating. He realized that somehow all the millions of steps, unendurable pain, and reparation leading up to his death could have been avoided at any other moment except this one.

Lowly Grillot Holt, Aaron's own familiar, spurted free from the hilt of his sword, plucked the weapon up, and ran its master through.

Oh my Christ.

Self shouted, *I told you that little bastard cheats!* He grabbed the baby and made a run for it, scampering over the rocks and leaping crevices. Uriel howled and Lowly Grillot Holt and the idolatry gave chase.

The Nephilim kept tightening its fists until even my father stopped laughing. The harlequin glanced over at me and I thought I saw the hint of recognition in his eyes. The heir of Armon drew its hands closer together, brought my dad and me face-to-face, and pressed us to its immense lips.

Nip sprang onto the mutant's cheek and

struggled to get the gigantic fists open, but we couldn't manage it. I didn't have enough air to tell him what to do, not that I had any ideas. Nip spun and charged up one of its nostrils, his claws kicking out and throwing sparks all over. The Nephilim cooed and eased its grip some.

Nip ran around inside its mountainous skull, giving it the intoxicating taste of doom it craved. Its hands opened farther and my dad and I fell onto the hybrid's unyielding belly. We barreled over the side and took a fifteen-foot header to the cave floor. I tumbled hard and my father landed on top of me. A couple of ribs on my left side broke as my shoulder dislocated. I screamed and Dad went "Woooo!" The Nephilim gave a stony sneeze and Nip came flying free.

Lowly Grillot Holt and the plastic saints had Self pinned upon the rocks. Elijah too, from inside the infant, fiercely fought against him. I knew he was having difficulty grasping tightly to the baby when all he could feel were barbs of malice from it.

Hold on! I said.

Stop telling me that in these kinds of situations! You ain't helpful at all!

I shoved my father off me and lurched to

my feet, feeling my left lung puncture. I grabbed his arm and pulled him along with me, afraid that he'd just start playing with the hybrid again.

Lowly Grillot Holt, bathed in the blood of his master and caught up in Uriel's zealotry, vaulted forward and managed to hook the infant's wrap in his talons. Self sank his fangs deep into Lowly Grillot Holt's throat, his tongue working inside the wound and gathering sustenance and power, sucking out the familiar's life, but it was already too late. Fane's and Catherine's daughter fell through the air. Only then, despite everything else, did the baby start to cry.

I dug in and sprinted toward them, listening to that single keening wail echoing around us. I watched the beautiful newborn bundle floating for an instant, as the nun had floated before spiraling to earth.

Eddie, showing no emotion, put his hands out, and the child almost landed safely in his arms. Almost.

Uriel's cloak flashed upward as he seized the girl, and held the baby over his head ready to hurl her down to the ground.

Gawain was close enough to clutch her, but he stood in his blind muteness, smiling in his pleasant manner, letting our world play out around him. Events, even matters like these, unfolded around him with equal value. Uriel closed his eyes in prayer and I shouted, "Don't!"

The baby's cry snapped in half and ended on a high note. A cloud of dust rose with my own scream.

Elijah's fury burst full-blown into the cavern and flew in delight at the covenant of being reborn. The heat of his lust blasted past me and blistered my cheeks. So much of his life and death had been focused on me and mine: his hatred, his desire for my love, his morbid suspicion and covetous nature. The energy wove around me as he sought out his new flesh, and it went roving toward the hybrid.

Covered with demon's ichor, Self sealed his mouth over the infant's. He was careful, so cautious in how he worked on her tiny dead form.

Save her!

I'm trying!

I went to my knees beside them and kept my hand on her tiny chest, holding in her ghost. Nip took Eddie's hand.

Don't stop, I ordered.

She's dead.

Keep at it.

He continued mouth-to-mouth resuscitation just as I'd been taught in the Boy Scouts. Her soul, already maimed by the force of Elijah's frenzy, fought to be liberated. It tried to find solace in a place that couldn't be called the afterlife, since she'd never lived.

It's not working.

Stop arguing with me!

I'm not! I'm just telling you!

I kept my burning hand on her cooling chest, the black crackling motes writhing around us. I could understand why she wouldn't want to live if this was a sample of what the world had to offer. Her flowing essence tried to drain through my fingers. Self breathed for her. Gawain took a step forward, drawn by purity.

My father—the lunatic murdered clown—had the respect not to laugh, though he smiled. Once he'd been proud of me, and himself, before his vanity kept him from bending his knee. He too had loved my Danielle, and talked of grandchildren. We'd planned for so long and had been so close to realizing our happiness.

This could have been my daughter if only I'd moved an inch to the right, awoken an hour earlier, not read a book, stayed a minute longer in confession, loved my woman a little more or perhaps a heartbeat less.

I was the Master Summoner, to the bone. If I could not invoke life, I could beckon hope.

The baby's fingers curled around mine.

"Praise be to God," Uriel said, and he sounded so sincere I wanted to break his spine. Self and I both dropped back gasping. The Nephilim's eyes flooded with Elijah, the empty windows of a vacant host suddenly welling with all his hatred.

Too fat from the richness of others' regrets, he had trouble sitting up. He had more occult might than ever before, but like a true newborn had virtually no control over himself.

His desire to kill me flared off him, superheating the cavern floor and turning the silicate to black glass. He still couldn't talk to me or express his love for Danielle, not with a Seraph tongue designed for timelessness. He remained trapped in his own way, and I couldn't help chuckling at that.

"Thy will be done, oh Lord," Uriel said. Elijah managed to turn over in his new form. His loathing and unending wrath were finally alive with him again. He roared with his rigid throat, crawled into the grotto, and allowed the waters to swallow him. He was still human enough to want to see Danielle raised on Oimelc, during the Feast of Lights, and Jebediah would promise him anything to ensure his service.

Elijah fell deeper and deeper into the muddy lake, giving me one last scornful leer before going to meet with his new coven to prepare for the second coming.

The baby cried and took in breath. Dad danced.

Gawain didn't come back with us through the dark. He sat in the dirt beside the body of Aaron, where the rock had been littered with playing cards and still glistened with the slithery viscera of Lowly Grillot Holt.

I kept staring at Uriel wondering if I should kill him, and do it with Aaron's sword. It might prove fitting. But it would be pointless. His role in these schemes and designs had finished playing out.

Instead I threw him down on Aaron's chest until his hands were covered with the blood of his brother.

Self had fun chasing down the plastic saints and stomping them flat.

Nip and Eddie still held hands. Eddie kept repeating, "I forget. I forget." The kid had been caught up in the maelstrom of confused men and even more confused gods, with his guts spilled out for everyone to poke through. I didn't know how to put him together again, but Nip and Abbot John would help.

I pulled the boy with no heart up from the murder hole, and Self followed cuddling the infant and singing French lullabies. My father stood at the pulpit and brayed like an animal or just a vicious sinner.

Abbot John had hanged himself in the chapel and swayed in the draft. He wasn't dead although he'd really been trying to kill himself this time. He just didn't have the affirmation for it.

I said, "Get off the rope, John. Your children need you. You'll like it in Cincinnati. Fane is going to show you how to sell shoes."

I helped him down from the noose and watched him shudder as he bowed in the pew. I handed him the jar with Eddie's heart and released the seven locks. He saw Uriel's wet hands.

When I told him the mount no longer had a reason to stand, he hissed with his ruined voice, "So now it begins."

I didn't want to hear a discourse on the conflicts of my life or his interpretation of events. My punctured lung grew worse until every breath rattled deep in my chest, exactly the same as when I'd arrived here seeking recovery. I slumped beside him into the pew and kicked up the kneeling rail.

"Meet him in the hills of Meggido," Abbot John whispered. "I saw it in a dream. Bring your armies."

"I have no armies. Neither does Jebediah. We're not the kings of the earth."

"Of course you are."

Of course we are, Self said. *Jerusalem calls. And Golgotha.*

It wasn't the truth—couldn't be the truth—but Jebediah believed it. Elijah and the new coven would reinforce his will and lend credence to his doctrine. He would not turn back for the sake of his rationality, not even on behalf of the world.

He'd drawn me into this war, and neither of us could carry on until our purpose was proven to be righteous or false. I sat thinking about Palestine and Mount Carmel, the ancient highways where invaders passed into the high point of the valley, built up over periods by the destruction and rebuilding of cities.

Self practiced his Hebrew, sounding almost happy. *Har Meggidon*.

Har Meggidon.

The mountains of Meggido, where the kings of the earth would meet.

Armageddon.

Part Three

Myself Am Hell

Chapter Thirteen

Like all wars, this one began with sacrifice.

Here, in a land of grudges and blood, Abraham had set out to murder his child. According to the Jews, the boy's name is Isaac. To the Muslims, it is Ishmael.

Untold thousands have died over such devotion to minor details and metaphor. Explosive devices are hidden under seat cushions because of mispronunciations. Entire families are poisoned for square inches at the back of a shrine or church. The Palestinians and Israelis fought over lines drawn in the dirt. Symbolism leads to suicidal missions inside wired trucks and boats. Women are stabbed for singing praises to a different god on a crooked street in the wrong quarter.

Where there is sanctity, there is Satan.

It's an ancient adage that fits the wide range of awe-inspiring faith and petty madness that is Jerusalem. It was easy to get preachy here.

The pink-haired lady, Betty Verfenstein, put it another way when she saw that I was watching the Muslims spitting on the Jews in the narrow alleys and labyrinthine bazaars of the Old City. The Jews were throwing rocks and everybody was screaming while the Israeli border guards hung back with their machine guns pointed down at the street.

"I couldn't care less what these fanatics do to each other," she said. "Except when I see children getting involved. They shouldn't have to grow up in this turmoil, all in the name of God. This isn't religion. I don't know what it is. I've never seen anything like it in my life." She planted her meaty fists on her thick hips and looked ready to outwrestle any of the squabbling well-dressed men. "All I'm sure of is that I wouldn't want any of them in my home during Passover."

There were dead children wrapped

around her throat, the silver psychic cords twining and whipping about her. Four miscarriages with broad flat heads and translucent, vein-packed skin, and her daughter, Theresa, who'd been murdered thirty-five years ago at the age of twenty.

Theresa had given me all the bitter details, seething in my ear on the plane. She'd been a sophomore at Yardale, cutting across the quad at night with her roommate on their way to a Phi Beta Kappa party, when the pine brush behind them suddenly came alive with arms and gray gloves. She still felt an intense loathing for her roommate, who ran off and left Theresa behind. Right there on one of the nation's safest campuses, in a spot surrounded by the windows to a hundred empty classrooms, she'd had her bowels carefully cut from her while her dead eyes watched each stroke of the fine blade and witnessed the slow and precise removal of her own internal organs. Still, all she saw were arms, and those unstoppable gray gloves.

Theresa wavered close, her teeth champed and white eyes wide now that she had finally come face-to-face with me.

My name had been carved in thin large

letters into her chest, years before I was born.

"You all right?" Betty asked. "You look a little sick."

"I'm fine."

She kept her gaze on the fighting. The sorrow etched itself deeper into each heavy line of her face, and the nervous tension kept her talking. "Manny's back at the hotel with heartburn. I wanted to go to Ecuador, but no, he wants to come see where the Bible was born. Except the water here is as bad for him as it was in Mexico. You and Manny, you're both going to be up all night."

Theresa continued to glare. Her open abdominal cavity showed that the butcher had only taken certain organs: the liver, the lower intestine, and part of her lower esophageal tract. The dried tissues could be used for divination. It reminded me of Eddie as everyone in the mount pulled together in order to replace his heart and put him back together again.

I could imagine Theresa's killer back then, with his gray leather gloves still on, surrounded with the burnt embers of her flesh and using a scrying mirror to stare into the future and see me at this exact moment. Why else would he have carved my name, unless he wanted to see my reaction?

I mouthed, *You'll pay for this*. I focused on him as well as I could, turning against the years that led toward Theresa's death. My mind roamed widdershins—counterclockwise—against the natural order of time. He watched me from the past. I could sense him there, grinning, so slick. He held his scrying mirror and looked deeply within it, staring, watching. He wanted a connection and he got it. I drew forth arcana and hid my glowing fists in my pockets. I recited a thricefold Assyrian hex and hurled a curse, feeling the tide flow against the very current of time. Thirty-five years ago it should've shattered the glass and sent the shards into the bastard's face, leaving him blind in at least one eye.

The miscarriages bobbed in front of us, snapping taut on the silver cords and then sluggishly wafting off. Theresa hissed and came at me with her fingernails poised to scratch my face to shreds. I didn't blame her. My second self unwound from my chest and stuck his chin out at her. *Hey! Who the hell do you think you are making faces like that?*

The wheel revolves. After haunting her

mother for so long, the girl now realized she'd been tortured and killed only to become the smallest part of a cruel pattern designed to rattle me. And worst of all—it hadn't. Theresa sneered.

Don't look down your nose at me! Self screamed.

Relax.

She started it! Stuck-up dead bitches are the worst.

"Did I tell you on the plane?" Betty asked. "With Manny's high blood pressure he's a prime candidate for a stroke. He retired two years ago and instead of making model airplanes or putting ships in a bottle he's been dragging me all over the planet ever since. All truth be told, I liked Japan more. Them Japanese are more respectful of other folks than this. Except during the big one, of course."

She'd told me on the El Al flight over, while Gawain and my father sat one row behind us. I had spent weeks going through a hundred obscure incantations but I still couldn't figure out how to strip the harlequin costume and dye from Dad's body. I called up all manner of majiks until my hands were singed and unfeeling. Self licked at the painted white face and black lips for hours as my father tittered like a schoolgirl on her first date.

Finally, I'd had to use pancake and foundation to cover his clown face just so I could get him on board the plane from JFK to Tel Aviv. I hid his jester's cap under a ten-gallon cowboy hat that made him look like a ludicrous version of Hoss Cartwright. The stewardess tried to get him to put it in the overhead compartment. Eventually she realized her mistake when he started doing a jig in the aisle and instigated a food fight onboard with the kosher deli trays.

I hadn't known how I was going to get them past customs, but I needn't have worried. Gawain and my father simply walked past all the Israeli officials while my luggage was checked and rechecked and I was held in a tiny white room for hours until they finally let me go.

Betty and Manny Verfenstein had taken to my father for some reason, perhaps because they thought he was the victim of a stroke.

I could understand it. Betty was nearing seventy and was boisterous and forthcoming about her life. Theresa filled me in on the rest as she dangled from her mother's throat, my name a wide-open wound. The cord's pressure sometimes made Betty gasp with pain as memories lashed against her.

She was a plump woman with crows'-feet stamped into every meaty angle of her features. She had buried her only daughter and the endless ache had worn down her faith but not her convictions. She had a defiant rough laugh that filled me with a pleasant warmth. It drove Self bugshit on the plane and made him crawl into the overhead compartments, where he rifled the baggage.

Eventually the fracas ended. A girl limped away crying with two badly skinned knees, comforted by her mother. This kind of scene would be repeated several times a day. Small skirmishes, shoving matches, and screaming arguments were punctuated by other, more savage violence. The leaders of nations from around the world had been vainly trying to get these people to talk peace for years. It had not worked in five millennia, and it never would.

It was Good Friday.

Betty shook her head sadly, and her daughter and the miscarriages twined above, swept aside by the dangling cords and coiling together. "This has nothing to do with the Bible."

She was wrong. It had everything to do with a book that had toppled empires and forged ten thousand wars. The letter and law of its lessons. Contradictions and prophecies held too much consequence, no matter what you believed. That was all they had left of God, and all they could imagine.

"Hope your father is enjoying himself," she told me. Another person might have said it with an air of sympathy, sincere or not, but Betty Verfenstein only spoke what she meant. "I've got to get back to Manny. You take care."

Theresa swung down low one last time, my name shining in her gutted flesh. Her ribs had chips in them from where the blade had sunk deep. She glowered, hissing and despising me, as she deserved to do. Even the miscarriages scowled and gave me the malformed finger.

Self shouted, *And you, you snooty chick, you're lucky I don't come up there and slap you around some.*

I left the Old City of Jerusalem and wandered the hills for the rest of the afternoon. Despite the fervor, you could find peace here, alone in the dirt. There was no wind. I stared out over the countryside and felt a welcoming embrace of heat and epochs.

Even with all of time sewn into Self's soul I found that he was hurrying ahead of me.

Self gazed about the rocky spur of the Judaean hills and laughed, listening to the mania of the land. As expected, all of Jerusalem, full of hostility and passion, echoed his wild happiness.

He was home.

Goddamn, it's good to be back.

I stared down at the city knowing that I should have come here a decade earlier with Danielle, back when my studies might have led to something with purpose and significance. Perhaps even discovery and revelation, at a time when I could have reveled in my belief.

Jerusalem, known in Hebrew as Yerushalayim, and in Arabic as Al Quds, was the center of worldwide credence and certainty. The reverend in Perdido, Alabama, owed his yellow pine altar to this far-off expanse of sand.

I spotted tufts of sallow, a willowlike shrub that supposedly has wept since the Jews' captivity in Babylon. Perhaps it was true. Nature not only reflects God, but history. Each moment is rooted in antiquity. The dead past never recedes, and remains as close now as ever. I had warded off

Oimelc, the Feast of Lights sabbat, only to face Lent in the place where Christ had been born, preached, died, and altered the rest of humanity.

Stop it, Self hissed.

What?

Running through it again changes nothing. I'm sick of hearing it. He held his hands over his ears as if I were shrieking into his face. The more sentimental and pensive I grew, the more he leaped around. *Quit it! Can't we just have some fun for once?*

It would be nice, I said.

Stop it then. Come on, these Israeli army chicks are firm, and they got handcuffs!

He watched the girls walking on the roads and whistled after them. He sighed and dreamed of bruised wrists, lapping at torn veins, and stroking dimpled kneecaps. My stomach tightened and my groin flooded with heat, and I went over sideways in the dust grabbing my guts. He grinned at me, the red sunset washing over his teeth so that it looked as if he had a mouth brimming with blood.

It wasn't his provocation but mine. It had the old familiar feeling. Temptation in the desert was not unknown.

Into this land came a man named

Yashua, a stoneworker—not a carpenter—who traveled from a small village to work in the cosmopolitan city of Galilee, during the time of the first zealots. There he learned of the rebellion against the tyranny of Rome, and grew aware of himself within a political tinderbox. He learned at the knee of a man who ate locusts and wild honey and dressed in camel's hair clothes. He returned home to Nazareth and was rejected by his own people, and was forced to start a new and active community with his own disciples.

Just as Jebediah had done.

Is he here yet? I asked.

You know, the fur-lined leather cuffs are just as nice. Twin straps.

It got like this on occasion, when he glided among my weaknesses and took advantage. *Is he here?*

Yes.

Why hasn't he made his play yet?

Who's to say he hasn't? His grin grew wider. In the coming darkness his mouth was no longer crimson but now hung open filled with moonlit fangs. *Why haven't you made yours?*

What the hell does that mean?

His smile dropped like a plum stone, and

218

he frowned at me. *You're asking the wrong questions.*

You deliberately being contrary?

Who, me?

The desert began to grow cold. I stood and headed down the hill. The coastal plain to the west led thirty-five miles to the Mediterranean, and to the east you could see the salt banks of the Dead Sea.

The New City portion of Jerusalem was quite modern, but due to a municipal ordinance all buildings were built with Jerusalem stone, providing a uniquely archaic and primitive aspect to the city. Its garden suburbs, broad avenues, and modern apartment buildings contrasted with the meager dwellings of the Old City.

I walked through the Dung Gate, located near the Western Wall. It was low and narrow. A great deal of the city's refuse was taken to the Kidron Valley by an ancient sewer that runs beneath the passage, giving the gate its name. I headed toward the center of town, past the Ben Yehuda mall, and back to the Jerusalem Tower Hotel. Self kept after the Israeli girls and said they all reminded him of the daughters of David. Long black hair curling in waves, features sharp yet somehow soft. He quivered as he rushed into the onset of night.

When I walked in the door to the hotel room, my father giggled and danced with the little bells of his garb ringing wildly. He bounded into my chest like a happy pet and wouldn't let go until I'd patted his back for a few minutes.

Gawain continued his blind vigil, regarding nothing but seeing everything in focus. I realized that he already knew how this would all end, and that he probably didn't really care one way or another.

He and my father, unworldly in their simplicity, could witness and smile at the unfolding of revelations. Gawain was still dressed in a lavender cloak, and his bleached white hair and pale face appeared to glow in the dimness of the room. The lights of Jerusalem opened over his shoulder through the windows.

He mouthed my name and reached for me. I took his hand, but he no sooner grasped it than he let go and moved away. Whatever guidance or warnings he had would remain locked inside him.

Self flipped the channels around past German, French, and Russian stations. With a frustrated snarl he started kicking the television. *I can't find* Friends, *damn it*.

The full moon rose over Israel, and my mother came to me again in the gulf of night, into my uncomfortable seat of dreams.

Dad seemed to feel her as well and sat on the floor whispering unintelligibly to himself. Whatever portion of his soul remained would be curled up in shame deep within the harlequin.

Even Self was unsettled. He trembled at the indistinct presence of my mother. He let out caterwauls in tune with Dad's whines and jingling, all of us lost beneath Gawain's endless sight and silence.

She moved as I remembered her, with a lissome balance as though the earth let her go for a moment as she walked, and then took her back again. She'd sit in the church basement teaching Sunday school, surrounded by a ring of children who didn't care about God or our sins or any kind of retribution. We only wanted to go outside to the lake or the park and play softball and try our hand at the rowboats, catching trout on string lines with wet balls of stolen communion wafer.

My mother understood the nest of shadows stirring behind the altar and between the pews. In spite of ourselves, she tried to prepare us for the inevitable. The priests began to scowl at her lessons and eventually dismissed her. She could read the word of the Lord with a clarity unmarred by ages of canon, doctrine, and ego. The hypocrisy of the Pharisees lives on.

My father's clownish face fell in on itself. The painted smile remained though his mouth didn't quite tug so far at the corners. He seemed to be trying to speak, or perhaps even sing, the way he did on the porch during summers when mother swept through the kitchen carrying icy beer out to him.

He leaned back against the headboard, one knee bent and his arm resting atop it, in the same pose as when he tilted his chair on the veranda. He'd sometimes strum his guitar or smoke hand-rolled cigarettes that made him go into sneezing fits. He understood what was coming but refused to be baited by it. He knew calm back then, short-lived as it was, before he started throwing rocks through the church's stained-glass windows.

I called to him once more, just as I had every day since leaving the mount, hoping to find my way to him again. "Dad?"

He didn't look at me, but his smile widened when Self flicked on to some music video program and they started dancing along to an Israeli pop band.

Familiars watched us, perched all across the city.

Every so often Self went on a hunt and brought some lower-tier imp back in his jaws or crushed in his fist. Two nights ago he returned to the room laughing and giving a piggyback ride to Elemaunder Pondo, who now took the shape of a baboon. Pondo had been handed down through the generations of the Lugbara family in Zambia, but the last tribal leader of the Candomble cult had died recently of AIDS. Pondo could not be controlled anymore and he traveled north across the continent, suckling at the teats of witches when he could. He climbed my shirt and tried to get at my chest, bouncing and screeching.

Self said, *Ain't no man-boy love for you there, buddy, try the Franciscans*. I scrawled a binding charm in front of Pondo's tiny face, and with his fur standing on end he got the point.

They watched television and made fun of everyone's accents. When they got bored they conjured a pair of dice and got up a game of craps in the corner with three shifty djinn. Self cleaned up and made a couple hundred shekels and sixty agorot. The coins and bills had been stolen from the wallets of men murdered in a bus bombing that afternoon. My father let loose with a bark of laughter, watching Pondo trying to make the six point.

The room was already filled with the dead. I could feel them pressing their determination toward us but I couldn't be sure of their intent. Bridgett with her throat slashed, those beautiful emerald eyes turned on me again as she grinned, knowing her place in the much larger pattern. I had survived Oimelc no better than an addict going cold turkey, thrashing and crawling on all fours in my need for Danielle. The desire for redemption had grown stronger each passing minute, year piled on year as my hair became tinged with gray. I had wept and vomited and smashed furniture. Once I'd awoken to find my father holding me in his arms, crying and cackling.

Pondo and the djinn all perked up in the same moment, glanced about the place, and began squawking. It looked as though they wanted to leave, but Self kept the game going, offering outrageous odds so they'd stick around. My hackles stood on end and a shiver went up my spine as if a wedge of ice had been pressed to the small of my back.

So, something was finally about to happen.

Blind Gawain grabbed my father by the hand and led him from the room. His serpent's tongue flicked out once toward me. Giggling, Dad waved and allowed himself to be dragged into the hall. The door slammed shut behind them and the room cooled by ten degrees.

I knew I was about to have a really bad night.

He's here, Self told me.

Who?

He isn't alone.

Who?

Shh.

We waited. Pondo started making a comeback and kept counting his money, which irritated the djinn. Self had to calm them all down before a fight broke out. It went on like that for a couple of hours, with the television blaring, the dice clicking, and coins ringing.

There was a knock at the door.

I turned to answer and stopped in my tracks.

A boy of nine stood inside the room. The skin on his face was puckered, disfigured, and discolored, and he had no hair on his head. His lips were gone and what little remained of his mouth didn't work all that well. There was only a tiny hole in the middle of all the seared flesh.

It took him a while to get anything out, but eventually he whispered, "The fireman is coming."

The child climbed onto the bed and crawled beneath the sheets, fading as he did so until only his outline was left in the blankets. The knocking grew more insistent.

Self said, *Don't answer that.*

Why not?

You don't want to know.

You're probably right.

Yes.

He tapped his foot in time with the beating of our hearts, waiting it out, his claws clacking together in a steady rhythm. He seemed puzzled, his brow furrowed, as if he were seeing me for the first time in his life. Then he shook his head in disappointment, looking so much like my father that his expression made me suck wind. Perhaps he'd taken so much from me that he finally just wanted to give some of it back.

Can't you just tell me? I asked.
Can't you ever just listen to me?

Another knock, much louder. I went to answer.

Fine, Self said. *Don't come crawling to me if you get burned.*

I opened the door.

Giant, dim Herod, who had greater power than even Jebediah had ever imagined, stood there ten years dead.

"How're you doin'?" he asked. "How've you been?"

"Herod," I whispered.

"You feeling okay?"

He'd lumbered around the covine tree that final morning, knowing how to laugh and love his enemies. He'd told us all that the invocations would go wrong. He'd wept on Danielle's shoulder, afraid to continue but unwilling to disappoint his friends. For ten years I'd been wondering why I hadn't listened to him.

"You been getting out of the room?" he asked. "You been seeing the sights?"

Herod, the fourth to die, with his eyes bleeding as he was swept backward with open arms, grinning a little while he plunged onto a limb of the covine tree and was run through. His heart had been pierced and dark blood spewed from his nose and mouth across his robes. He'd still held out on the hope of meeting God and being forgiven for all the sins his parents had beaten into him.

"That Pondo over there? Hey, Pondo, long time no see, man. You making some cash? You think you can float me a fifty until payday?"

Herod had been chained in a fruit cellar until he was fifteen years old. He'd learned about life from rats, roaches, and spiders in that time. He'd believed the insane screams of his mother when she branded the devil from him. He was saved by the ministering spirit Reschith Hajalalim and the angel Masleh as his father tried to fight them off with a fireplace poker. I could still see the soldering iron scars on Herod's throat.

He nodded once to me, as if he'd just run out for a six-pack and had returned to watch a ball game. He pawed his sweaty neck and said, "Ah, feel that, fucking amazing, you've got air-conditioning. Mind if I come in?"

I stepped out of his way. Pondo crapped out and stamped his feet.

Herod shrugged with a sidelong glance. "You're wondering about the change, I see.

Well, don't. I can tell you things now that I couldn't then."

He not only teemed with intelligence but he was smooth now, a real schemer. He spoke in the rapid-fire cadence of a used car salesman making a pitch.

"Who are you?" I asked.

"Hey, you know me, c'mon now, what kind of question is that? Listen, you've got to listen to me, I've been meaning to tell you something for a long time but I couldn't before. You'll be grateful for this, really. You know who I am."

Maybe I did.

A little help over here? I called.

Six straight passes! You handle it!

Herod moved with his usual awkward gait, lumbering about as if he might fall at any second. When he got in front of the air conditioner he stood there letting the streams of cold air wash over him. "You're going to cause more trouble, aren't you? Yeah, you are. You might be one of the kings of the earth but you're still a goddamn sap."

"Sounds like you've got issues."

"A few, I suppose. Some things you never get over."

"I'd agree with that."

229

"Of course you would. But that doesn't matter now. Listen, listen, don't take this wrong, but I think you're going to die here in the dust."

I couldn't yet tell who wore the mask of Herod's flesh. I kept my hands low at my sides and scrawled protective sigils of Machon, Raquie, Sachiel, and Caffiel against my legs.

Jebediah enjoyed playing games with the dead. My father's return, the threat and promise of Danielle being raised, and this whole ludicrous notion of resurrecting Christ proved how much fun he had toying with souls. I tried to get Self's attention but he ignored me.

Little Joe! Papa needs a new Benvenuto Cellini Rolex with sapphire crystal glass and applied Roman numerals with a crocodile skin strap!

"I can make sure you come out on top this time," Herod said, beginning to show irritation. He couldn't quite catch his breath as he continued to sweat. Veins pulsed in his neck, making the scar tissue throb. "There's no need for you to keep being anybody's whipping boy."

"Who in particular?"

"It's all right," he said, fuming. His frenzy

came across in full blossom now as he
swayed on his feet. The words erupted in
bitter bites and he gagged on them. "I'm not
mad at you anymore." His eyes bulged,
straining free of the sockets. "You did what
you had to do. That's completely understandable. Really. Don't worry about it. Listen, listen, I forgive you."

"For what?"

"I can help you." He showed his unbal-
ance in a rictus smile. Sweat poured off his
face, droplets catching in those thick eyelashes. A mop of sopping hair stuck against
his wet forehead. He was generating serious heat. "This is gonna sound a little out
there, but listen, listen. Hey, I . . . I love
you!"

Sparks and ribbons of bile suddenly ran
from his lips. His teeth started to break
apart. His clothes began to crawl. Coat and
trousers distended and ballooned, full and
creeping. Ebony motion rippled and peered
out from his cuffs, between his shirt buttons, now dropping to the floor.

Salamanders.

They swung their tails, already spraying
neurotoxins from their poison glands as he
began to ignite and plumes of smoke rose
from him in a hundred places. Black and

yellow striped creatures swarmed from him.

Griffin. It was Griffin.

The only man I'd ever killed in hate, but in death he'd forgiven me.

Now Griffin's malice was much more alive than he was. I could feel the rage burning as he let it out toward me, thinking of the children with leukemia that he'd roasted to death. He laughed. He was always laughing.

His murder was the worst thing I'd ever done without feeling any regret.

He had loved Jebediah in life but he'd been a slave to his own pyromania. He spoke as if he'd been sent here to help me. What kind of discoveries had the firebug made in the flames of hell?

"Griffin, you forgave me."

"I have!"

"Why this now?"

"I love you!" he shrieked. "He loves you! He is your child, you are his child!"

"Yeah, right."

"You must listen—"

I would've if he'd made any sense. The fires spurting from him had me a little jumpy. "How do those fingers work for you?"

"What?"

"Those fat bulky hands." Herod couldn't even hold a drinking glass without shattering it. He couldn't use silverware or pet a dog. He killed whatever he dared try to caress. Those enormous fingers twitched. "Must be damn near impossible to light a match."

From an ashtray on the nightstand I grabbed a book of matches with the hotel name on them and lit one. Griffin's eyes, already loose and quivering, danced madly, the same way they had the night he came back from burning down the children's hospital. I blew out the match and he let loose with a squeal of frustration.

"Who sent you?"

"Nobody."

He could be playing semantics. Half the demons in hell were called "no body" or "nothing" or Beliya'al, meaning "without worth." If there was any possibility that Jebediah's demented plans had to do with Armageddon, then all the dukes and lords in Pandemonium might be ready to assist him, despite their general disgust to truck with headstrong witches.

"Who called for you?"

"You did—"

"Why have you revoked your forgiveness? Are you in service to Jebediah?"

"Are you? Are you? Listen here—"

I preferred Griffin's hate to the machinations of some hidden will. He'd been murderously insane but it was a human madness, driven by a human perverse need. Who could have the power to bring Herod's body back and stuff it with the fiery heat of Griffin? And why?

"I want a name," I said.

He was desperate for some kind of release, jittering as the salamanders swarmed over and through and inside him. "I know you do."

"Why've you come back?"

"To tell you a secret, you prick!"

The fireman was fast, and he sprang at me.

He had Herod's body but none of his strength. Flailing, he splashed the room with neurotoxins, the salamanders sticking to the walls. I reached into his chest and squeezed my fist on things that slinked and burned. They poured free of him, squirming from his mouth, out his nose. They shoved aside his eyeballs to clamber down across his distended cheeks. And still he smiled.

"What secret?" I shouted. "Griffin, tell me!"

The djinn had been born in fire, but Pondo wasn't waiting around any longer to see what happened. He grabbed up his cash and made it out the window, and the game broke up.

I'd waited too long.

Salamanders fled under my feet, furious and full of loathing. Like all witches, Griffin believed in irony and symbolism, and the creatures kept leaping to burn my left side in the same place where I'd stabbed him to death. Dozens became hundreds as they dropped from the ceiling and crawled into the drains, a thousand slithering amphibians roiling with inferno.

I was on fire.

Smoke swirled and filled the room. Alarms sounded. My spells and hexes broiled and fractured into pieces. I turned for the door but Griffin lurched forward and held on, even as Herod's corrupted corpse blazed into more salamanders. Poison spewed into my face. My own screams deafened me as my skin bubbled and incinerated, the flames destroying tissue and burning down to the fat, muscle, and bone. The black tissues shredded away. Rolling in

235

excruciating pain, gritting my teeth, I looked up to see Self calmly sitting atop the television.

He only stared at me.

Herod's body wasted away as the salamanders continued to burst from the rags of his clothes. I tried to scream again but couldn't get it out as my vocal cords boiled away. The torture was unbearable.

Burning, I crawled to Self.

Help me!

I do, Self said. *I did*.

Please!

You sure? he asked. He cocked his head and looked down at this mess, his features so similar yet different from mine, completely unreadable even to me. *You positive you want my help?* He wanted me to beg some more even as I was lost beneath a tide of flame, but I couldn't ask again, even as my seared corneas ripped off against my eyelids. He thought about it for a moment before saying, *Of course*.

Invocations flooded his frame. He gripped me by the wrist and yanked me from the room, more layers of my skin coming off in his claws. There wasn't any pain anymore because all my nerve endings were gone.

He pulled me down the empty corridor. It was easy for him because I weighed no more than eighty charred pounds now.

Clambering up my back, Self licked along the length of my spine, cuddling and cooing as I moaned and sobbed, magic coursing along his radiant hands, stroking the wounds. He spit on me and cooled the burns. I cried out and tried not to bite through my tongue from the torture. I couldn't help it though and my mouth flooded with blood as the damaged tissue grew back and my nerves sang with agony. Self nuzzled my throat, his charms mending me as I held back screeches, ligaments and muscles rebuilding. My eyes healed and I could see again.

He kept working, restoring me with his gentle, loving touch.

Come on, let's go.

The entire building was in flames now as the salamanders ran freely through the hotel, spewing fire. Naked, I held on to Self's hand and followed him out through the billowing smoke. Somewhere along the way I got lost in the thick haze. He seemed to shake me off, and I lunged for him, grabbing hold again. It wasn't until I was outside that I saw I was clutching on to a man's sleeve.

He was clearly Greek, with curly black hair salted with white, clean-shaven, and teeming with the power of epochs. I'd been burned enough for one night. I stepped away from him, my eyes still tearing, and when my vision cleared enough I saw that he was only a dying old man.

The plowed lines of his face ran to dark trenches that cut so deeply he seemed to have been sliced open with a nail file. His mouth hung slack and his lips were a sickly gray. He was trembling so badly I thought he'd fall over and die in my arms, but he held his ground, regarding me carefully, and slowly backed off.

"Who are you?" I asked.

"A companion in tribulation," he said, and was gone.

Chapter Fourteen

I walked the Via Dolorosa at dawn.

Dominated by the Temple Mount, called the Haram by the Muslims, the Old City was split into separate quarters: Christian, Muslim, Jewish, and Armenian. Churches showed the architectural touches of the Byzantine and Crusader eras. Eight gates in the wall of Suleyman the Magnificent opened to the smell of spices and the sound of *meuzzins* calling Muslims to prayer.

Along with hundreds of others, I'd spent hours last night outside the hotel watching the firefighters and rescue crews battle the blaze. They carried out the wounded and the dead by the dozens. Someone covered me in a sheet and police questioned me at length. The investigators wouldn't be able to determine that the fire originated in my room. The salamanders had scattered flames all across the building so that it went up simultaneously on several different floors.

They cared a great deal about my passport. Members of the American Consulate appeared and asked more questions and made assurances. I was given a gratis room in a different hotel. Somebody brought me some clothes that didn't fit and Self handed over his poker money so I could get some that did.

Now I stood before the Golden Gate, called the gate of mercy, which is situated on the eastern wall of the Temple Mount. It was sealed by the Turks hundreds of years ago because of Jewish tradition that the messiah would return through it after traveling from the east over the Mount of Olives. Now it opened toward the mount and the Garden of Gethsemane. Self stared into the distance as if he could see Jesus walking toward us through all of history.

He sniffed and said, *He came this way.*
Christ?
Herod. And Griffin.

And Jebediah, I was certain. He wouldn't have been able to pass up this place of murder. King Solomon's Temple stands alongside the tile Muslim mosque called the Dome of Rock. Archangel Gabriel carried Muhammad to heaven from there. It's also the place where Abraham prepared to sacrifice his son. Jebediah would have pressed his forehead to the ground, dreaming of an exposed throat offered before heaven, the curved blade edging into the child's skin.

Power calls to power, blood to blood.

David captured the city from the Jebusites in 1000 B.C. It had been conquered and destroyed by everyone from Nebuchadnezzar to Hadrian. There was more bone in this dust than in any other place in the world, and men like Jebediah could put it to use.

Men like him and me.

Israeli flags flew in the Muslim quarter as Jewish Fundamentalist Nationalists gained a foothold by moving into houses in that part of town. The wailing wall comprises the western retaining wall of Solomon's Temple, the only remaining structure still standing from the original shrine. It is the holiest of sites, say the Jews, for it is there where the living God remains.

I could feel the energy throbbing in the stone, but whether from God or from the shrieking faith of misled men, I didn't know.

North of the Haram is the Via Dolorosa, the Way of Sorrows, where Jesus dragged the cross into Calvary. It ends at the Church of the Holy Sepulcher, erected by Constantine, the first Christian Roman Emperor, and built over the site of Golgotha, the place of the skull, where Christ and thousands of other men were crucified. To the east of the church is Gethsemane, in which he was kissed by a betrayer and the soldiers came for him while his disciples slept. Jebediah would like the idea that the land itself was tainted with treachery. In his own fashion, he had quite the Christ-complex. So did I.

The bazaars were already busy, the city awake and bustling, selling meat and vegetables, leather, jewelry, pottery, and perfume. The sun was strong and beat down harshly against my fresh pink skin. There was no wind.

Self kept trying to peek under skirts, the heat working on him as well. His thoughts kept veering, circling through the ages, from hell's bedlam to his growing need to lash his tongue against the succulent wound of a torn thigh. My fingers trembled. Nausea swept in low, and within seconds grew so bad that I nearly doubled over.

I said, *Stop,* and he merely looked at me. *What's that?*

Quit dreaming of blood.

Say again?

Of red bellies . . .

I'm not.

. . . and ripped knees, the taste of pale—

I'm not, he said, sounding calm and perhaps even concerned. *You are.*

My fingers kept twitching as the smiles of women turned toward me and then turned away again. A tic in my neck kept going for another minute as sweat coursed though my regrown eyebrows. The nausea finally faded.

You all right? he asked, looking so much like me that I didn't know where I was— here staring at him or over there gazing back at someone just as familiar.

I glanced into my palm and saw that my new hand had a different lifeline that could barely be seen. I wondered how much of this remade body had been born from him.

Come on, I said.

Not the stations of the cross. They're so

friggin' boring. And besides, Golgotha calls.
Of course it does.

I walked the Way of the Cross. Scholars argued the actual path—even if the Via Dolorosa wasn't it, enough blood had been spilled here to make Self overjoyed. He dove and rolled in the streets, licking the ancient stone and drinking eras until his drool was as black as the lost epochs. Like a child let loose in a candy shop, he soon grew sick to his stomach.

This place gives me the creeps.
Me too, actually.

I could almost hear the loud, ugly scraping sound of Christ dragging his cross along these stones toward Golgotha, now the Church of the Holy Sepulcher.

There seemed to be as many tourists as there were citizens of the Old City. Heads bowed, hands clasped, their song swelled for a moment and then droned on.

Emperor Constantine the Great had a church erected on this site in A.D. 325. The buildings were destroyed and rebuilt several times through the centuries. Christians—especially Catholics and Greek Orthodox—believed that Christ was crucified on this spot and buried here. Many Protestants conjectured that Jesus

was crucified on the hill near the Garden
Tomb and buried nearby.

I don't want to go in there.

You just said that Golgotha calls.

It does. For you, not me.

Are you so sure?

I'm gonna get myself a latte.

The church was vast, with many rooms,
chapels, murals, and holy areas. I entered
the enormous main building, expecting a
vast pulse of divine might, or at least a wave
of psychic energy, but there wasn't much of
either. Perhaps that meant something, or
perhaps not. Maybe at its heart this church
was no different from any other in the
world. I walked along through the chambers and stood before the Chapel of the
Nailing on the Cross, also known as the
Eleventh Station.

People roamed and whispered. Tourists
videotaped the high walls, the altars, and
the other faithful as if expecting them to
perform in some way. Here were the meeting of the shallow and the mystical, eyes
filled with awe and other vacuous gazes. I
didn't know what to expect here or what I
might be longing for. Perhaps I'd only come
because Danielle had spoken of visiting. It
was as honest a reason as any.

A woman knelt at the altar in the chapel. I was about to leave when she turned to me and said, "Have you no idea where you are?"

"Yes, I do."

"Then don't you believe you should kneel?"

Many others sat or stood in the chapel and throughout the church, but she'd singled me out. Her voice was soft, without an edge despite the rigid words.

I knelt beside her. It had been a lifetime since I'd truly prayed. Not stating the demands of invocation or the rage of incantations, but offering simple prayer. It felt almost beyond me now. My thoughts were muddled and suddenly my heart began to hammer.

Prayer never gave me any kind of strength. Instead it allowed all my frailty and weaknesses to surface. On my knees was when I wanted the most from God, and when my greed surged inside me and I felt the most neglected. I deserved something for my sacrifices. I had no need for yet another penance—the last ten years of my life had been nothing but one long atonement.

She saw I was having trouble and reached out to grasp my arm. It was a friendly but strong touch. She squeezed once and let go. I clasped my hands together until my knuckles cracked and my fingernails drew blood. I could hear nothing but my own empty pleas, begging for the return of my love and a second chance at redemption.

How could anyone kneel here in the place of the skull, where Christ himself had died in agony at the hands of his enemies, while his screams were ignored by his own father, and somehow expect God to listen to you?

Red bellies, and the pale taste of—

Perhaps it was fear or some other force, but I got off my knees with a savage heave.

"If you don't believe, then why are you here?" she asked.

"I do believe."

"Then it must be your pride that makes you so uncomfortable?"

She spoke with a slight Greek accent. Six Christian communities shared the Church of the Holy Sepulcher. The Greek Orthodox were the landlords who rented this holy space by the inch. The Egyptians and Syrians leased a small section by the tomb. The Armenians had been here since A.D. 300, and the Catholics since the Crusades. The Ethiopians lived in a small monastery on the roof, and during Easter, while the others pushed and shoved each other here, they would dance and sing up there, without vanity or pride.

I was starting to get a little annoyed. "Why are you asking?"

"In this chapel, you must have no conceit."

"Believe me, lady, if it's one thing I don't have, it's conceit."

"The very fact that you should say such a thing proves you are a slave to it."

She had lengthy black hair held back in a shawl, with cloudy dark eyes carrying the weight of other people's pain. I could imagine she came from a large family that had fought in uncountable wars across endless deserts. She may have buried her brothers or her husband or her father, but someone who had died for his faith.

Or perhaps I was wrong and she was simply tired of working in the bazaar all morning, as she struggled to gather herself together enough and return home to ill parents or a crying infant.

She swept aside her hair in a gesture that reminded me so much of Danielle that I felt a painful pull in my gut. She stared at me with a puzzled expression, but not an unkind one. Her head tilted and she blinked once, twice, not quite frowning but almost there. My breath grew shallow and I realized I was blushing. I looked away but she didn't, and after a moment I glanced at her again.

I wondered if she'd reach to touch me once more, but she didn't. The stirring warmth became an almost soothing sense of arousal, here in the spot where the hammers rang against the spikes being driven into the flesh of Christ.

She rose, crossed herself, and stared at me a long final moment before she turned on her heel and walked up the aisle and out the chapel.

I waited for a while as the shadows twined across the floor and flashless cameras clicked and buzzed all around. My shoulders tightened and began to sag. My own dead past had a particular weight all its own whenever something hunted me down and came across me again.

The scent of fresh-cut pine and sweet balms swept up from behind, and I knew I'd been found.

"You aren't about to consider starting a romance now of all times, are you?"

It was Fane.

He looked obscene without his robes, so nervous in his identity as a man now, and not a monk, that I almost felt sorry for him. It isn't easy coming back to the world. The martyr played heavily in his face, but now there was a reason for it. He'd been subsumed by the role he'd once played.

The pine splints around his legs poked out at odd angles beneath his trousers. He'd let his Vandyke grow out into an unkempt bush, but there were still the remnants of the two sharpened prongs hanging off the end of his chin. He'd become gaunt, and walked cautiously as if he might be knocked down from any direction. I knew the feeling. An odd swirl of odors enveloped him. He still enjoyed bathing in heavy oils, and he'd taken advantage of several Middle Eastern balms and ointments.

Perhaps he'd come to learn that history could not be parceled out. Every breath had its consequence. He still didn't have the conviction of a soldier of God, but I could tell that the events on the mount had given him a new purpose. Of everyone on Magee Wails, he might well be the only one who'd actually gotten something beneficial from the destruction of the order.

"I was sure you'd go back to selling shoes in Cincinnati."

"That's why you so often make such significant mistakes. You really have no judgment of character."

"I'm beginning to believe you're right. How is Cathy?"

"Doing well."

"And Eddie? And the baby?"

"Eddie has fully recovered after his ordeal on Armon. Cathy named our baby Jean, after her grandmother."

"I'm glad everyone is fine."

He took another step closer and I could tell he wanted to get into it. "A month ago when I saw you last you had a small scar at the edge of your left eye. Now it's gone." He peered at me more closely. "How can you ever learn from your mistakes when you don't even carry your own scars?"

"Do you really want to get into a conversation about wounds seen and unseen, and lessons that ought to be learned?"

Despite his failings, Fane was a scrapper and wasn't about to back off. "Your life is full of ghosts."

"Isn't everybody's?"

He appeared surprised that I should think so. "No."

"Enough of this. Is John with you?"

"He's dead."

I grimaced and let out a groan. Red lights blinked on camcorders pointed in our direction. I drew sigils and threw a hex so they'd get nothing but static. My anger welled and I reached behind me to scratch at the stone wall of the chapel. I wished for some vision or message to come down through the rock, and to be heard in the murmur of the two millennia since Christ perished.

"He didn't hang himself either," Fane said. "He left the mount with Janice and me and our family, and we went to Ohio. I don't know what he intended to do there or what kind of life he was hoping to find. I'm not sure I could've learned to sell shoes again, but I was willing to try. His third day in Cincinnati he was run over by a cab. If you laugh I'll kill you."

He'd drawn a stiletto and had the point wedged under my ear.

I thought about breaking his arm in three places, but this melodrama only proved that he'd loved the abbot deeply, and I sort of admired him for it. Irony mattered just as much to a witch as symbolism, and it was never anything to laugh at.

"Your judgment isn't very good either, Fane."

"I know," he said, pulling his one nice trick so that his voice came down from all around, high near the church ceiling. "It's true." The words swung between us, circling and swimming. Along with them came the distant echoes of his out-of-control Harley, the shattering glass, and a woman's shrieks.

He put his blade away and I wondered if he ever wearied of hearing those noises that had set him on his course, the way that I tired of listening to mine.

I asked, "Is Uriel with you?"

"No, though I suspect he's in Israel. Without his brother, his familiar, or his . . . 'god' . . . I don't expect him to enter the conflict."

"Don't be so sure."

"I'm not, really, but in his eyes he's already fulfilled his greatest purpose."

"I suppose he has," I said.

Fane had more on his mind but he didn't know how to come out with it. He hobbled forward, awkward as an infant just learning to walk. The terrible pain was evident in his face. He must've just broken his legs again within the last few days, maybe the first minute he stepped foot into the Holy Land.

Whispering, he asked an odd question. "Do you ever get worried?"

Sometimes you can be prepared for absolutely anything, except sincerity. "Why are you here, Fane? There's nothing you can do, one way or the other."

"I'm trying to keep the world from ending. If this truly is Armageddon—"

"It's not."

"You *are* worried. I can hear it in your voice. And you've every right to be. Before Abbott John left Magee Wails he had a dream about you."

"He told me."

"No, he had another vision. One that involved you and the archangel Michael."

Michael who would slay the red dragon with seven heads, ten horns, and seven crowns and save the world.

I said, "Involved us how?"

"He said Michael was trapped. I don't know what that meant, but the abbot believed you were supposed to free him."

"Abbot John was a good man, in his own way, but he was insane. After all that suffocation his brain was oxygen starved."

Fane was still edgy and tried to get the stiletto at my throat again, but I caught his wrist and easily bent it backward. Still, he wouldn't let go of the blade. "Your order doesn't hold much credence with me, Fane, considering recent events."

"Armageddon is upon us. The signs are occurring."

"Crap. You're putting too much faith in that book."

"And you too little."

I shoved him away and thought about it.

John of Patmos, author of the Apokaylpsis, the book of Revelation, and who called himself a companion in tribulation, was an extremist who kept the floundering Christian religion alive with fear of the apocalypse during a time of rampant paganism. His book was a letter written to the seven churches in Rome's eastern empire of Asia Minor, telling them to endure the worsening conditions for Christians under the Roman persecution.

Some preached his prophecies to be literal while others believed the book concealed his message in symbols and imagery, a message that couldn't be deciphered without some lost key to the original subtext. The truth, if it existed, might lie somewhere between. Or it might not.

I hissed into his face. "Do you expect the

sun to become black as a sackcloth of hair, and the moon to become blood, and the stars to fall from heaven?"

"There is no wind."

I swallowed, spun around, and just then saw Theresa floating above us with the silver cord flapping hard against the windows. My name on her chest stood out as clearly as if it still ran with her warm blood. She clawed at the air, trying to get closer. I brushed Fane aside and went to her, but she was already moving off, reeling with her arms outstretched to me as she slipped farther and farther away.

Fane took a step forward and nearly fell into my arms. "There's no wind because the four great angels hold the four winds in the corners of the world."

Maybe it was true, but I'd never much believed in Revelation because so few angels were spoken of by name.

"The apocalypse is already in motion," he said.

"And has been since the beginning of time."

"Abbot John said—"

"Do you really believe that my actions, or yours, might somehow alter the will of God?"

"We all must fulfill our fates."

I burst out laughing. It was a deranged and lonesome sound in the Church of the Holy Sepulcher, in the place of the skull.

Perhaps no one had laughed here in thousands of years—perhaps never.

And I couldn't stop.

Chapter Fifteen

Holding a cup of sweet Muslim coffee, Self found me in the streets. He was eating stolen Easter cookies, traditionally shaped like crowns of thorns. Crumbs speckled his lips, but still somehow reminded me of blood. *Glad you're having such a good time*, he said. *What's so funny?*

Nothing. Have you seen my father or Gawain?

Heard Pop's bells ringing a couple of times but I never caught sight of him.

He finished his spiced coffee with one large slurp and started to head back toward the bazaar for more. I stepped in his way and he glanced up curiously, with only the hint of his teeth showing. We'd come so far together and yet had hardly moved at all. The spices worked at the back of my throat, flooding my sinuses. Sugar coated my tongue, those cookies fresh and still warm in my stomach. He understood so much at times, knowing what he shouldn't. Other important concerns didn't matter to him at all.

My second self climbed up my shirt, perched on my shoulder, clambered over my head, and leaped to the ground where he ran off to find more coffee. I followed and watched while he stole a cup from a street stand. I tried not to enjoy the taste of it too much while he hummed to himself in delight.

Where's my father?

I don't know.

Tell me.

You don't listen very well.

I reached out to him then for some reason, and in the same second he held his hand out to give me a cookie. My new skin was red and looked raw and bleeding in the sun. I noticed his lifeline was much different from mine now, and I wondered if one of us was going to die soon.

Try to keep that happy mood, Self said. He

nodded east, toward the Mount of Olives. *Jebediah's arrived with his brood. They're waiting for you.*

Any suggestions?

He actually seemed to think about it. *Let's leave this goddamn dusty place to the zealots and head for Jamaica.*

I only wish.

He stomped a nice calypso beat, slowly at first before really swinging into it. He was good. I could almost hear the kettle drums and conch shells. *Come on, da ganja do you good, mon.*

We headed for Mount Olivet, toward the central summit, which was regarded as the Mount of Olives proper and where Jebediah would undoubtedly be expecting me in the Garden of Gethsemane.

I was still weak from the fire, and the walk emptied me further as sweat ran through my hair and dripped down the backs of my arms. Soon I felt as if I'd spent all morning in a sweat lodge ceremony and yet hadn't been cleansed. There was no balance or tranquillity in it. The nausea returned, vicious but fleeting, and I was forced to my knees in order to ride the sickness out.

Faith meant everything now, even if the

reasons for it were unknown. When the queasiness passed I stood and continued to climb the hills. The interminable silence was broken only by my footsteps and the occasional passing tourist bus. Self kept practicing his Jamaican accent and mimicking the booming laughter of huge island black men. I could feel the knotted mass of my thoughts and emotions unraveling into perfectly spun threads. Where could Michael be trapped and how could I find and release him? Who had the power to control the archangel that would champion the earth? Who had sent Griffin? And could I possibly resist the temptation to raise Danielle again?

Self said, *Mon, we get dat good roadside jerk chicken and steamed callaloo, and listen to dem drums! We gonna dance! We dance all day long and into da dark night!*

Who's here? I asked.

He gave the only answer he could, grinning while he pranced. *Everyone who needs to be*.

And there at Gethsemane, in the Grotto of Agony, where Iscariot had brought the soldiers and placed his kiss upon the betrayed,

I looked up to see the stoic disfigured face of Jebediah DeLancre.

His hair had grown almost completely silver and white, and those mismatched lips, forever melded into a sneer, looked like the kind of mouth that might have kissed Christ and led him to his death. The moon caught the exposed shard of yellow canine so that it glinted like a fang. He wanted to be beautiful again, and his vanity had led him to work on new spells to rid himself of the ugly stretches of scar tissue. They hadn't helped. He plucked at his goatee, which was also white.

Even now, as he aimed toward ruling the earth, he seemed less than half the man he'd once been. He would never get over the loss of his familiar, Peck in the Crown, or forgive the Sephiroth that had purified and ushered it into heaven. I no longer got any satisfaction from his suffering. His glare forever held fury, righteous loathing, and incredible overconfidence, but there were also traces of loss and transgression in his eyes.

Here, for the moment—this was his temple.

The members of his new coven milled about. They had names but no identities, growing to function as a single conflicted essence. Six men and five women, victims and victimizers, almost interchangeable as they moved through the garden. I could see that he'd snatched them from the world already rotted. They stank of murder, prison, and asylums. He'd learned after his first coven, after using and destroying us, that innocence and naiveté had capability too, and it was a potential he could not completely control. He'd learned from his mistakes.

Still, they were young, the same way we'd once been. Their faces were vain and arrogant and enraptured in the mystical lore and texts they'd unearthed. I had difficulty telling one set of features apart from another because they shared so much in common.

The marks of a variety of demons branded them already, and their familiars played in the garden and ran around my ankles. I recognized the jackdaw Hotfoot Johnson and the black owl Prickeare, the imps Vinegar Robyn and Mr. Broadeye Sack. The fat legless spaniel called Jamara, having once been lord of North Pandemonium and leader of sixty legions, worked itself like a slug over my shoes. Even at the bottom of hell there are still lower depths.

Uriel sat among them, desperately holding on to Aaron's sword, empty of its traitorous familiar. He'd torn most of his hair and beard out so that thick welts and scabs crosshatched his broad, sorrowful face. Perhaps he was a martyr for his god, or simply another lunatic. His porcelain figurines, plastic saints, and wooden statuettes lay broken but carefully propped up near his feet. He still needed his dolls.

He'd slid his hands over the blade so often that he'd cut the fingers of his left hand down to their last knuckles. The nubs were freshly cauterized.

When he looked up I knew he didn't see me at all. He whimpered, "Thy will be done, oh Lord, thy will be done." He'd said it so often since killing his brother that the words had lost all meaning, even for him. His voice was strained and sounded as dead as Aaron. I thought he probably hadn't said anything else to anyone since the caves beneath the mount, repeating his one plea to God as if that could save him.

Jebediah's other murdered coven wafted past, eager for their fulfillment and vengeance. If he'd sent Griffin against me, then he might possibly control the others. Jebediah himself didn't have enough respect for the dead that one needed to beckon them back at will, but he knew enough to toy with souls and reanimation, and always surrounded himself with ghosts.

I looked around at the new coven thinking there might be a new necromancer among them. Sweat stung my eyes as the faces of the living and the deceased swam, blended, and merged.

The stench of the atrocities they'd committed rose from them like vapor. I smelled Fuceas among the women and realized the demon earl had impregnated his eggs in two of them, just as he'd stuffed Janus with his yoke. They were hardly more than girls really, not even yet out of their teens. They stood together with their bloated bellies nearly touching, unsure of how they should greet me. They each gave a bizarre little curtsy.

They all used the olive grove like the altar beside the covine tree, circling but not quite fully aware of each other. They weren't a true coven, in balance and harmony with the earth. Even their evils did not fully mesh. Unlike our own covendom, this was not a place for witches. For martyrs, of course, and for the dissidents and the faithful, but not for us. They all knew it too, especially Uriel, looking toward Jebediah for some kind of authority that would make them potent here. I could see death in their eyes already, and couldn't get past the fact that Jebediah was about to slay yet another assembly of his followers.

Even as a ghost, Bridgett enjoyed touching the slain as much as she had when she was alive. She wove among Rachel and Janus, wanting the spawn of Fuceas for herself.

Self found her there and, almost shyly, crept closer to her as she knelt before him and allowed him to scale her chest. Her blond hair still had those two sweeping curls crab-clawing into her mouth, and he used his tongue to sweep her ringlets back. Her slashed throat still poured psychic energy, and he nuzzled the stream, kissing and licking her neck, trailing his fingers against her thighs. Like his mother, Thummim, he swung from Bridgett's left breast, suckling the witch's shriveled teat, which was filled with just as much syrupy milk as before. Her piercing green eyes cut toward me, features still containing some of the love of the novitiate she'd once been.

"Hey, lover," she said.

The incensed ghosts of the triplets Diana, Faun, and Abiathar, their lips still wet with wine, faded in and out around the Franciscan flower gardens. None of us could get away for our own past, not even the dead.

As I'd done so many times before, I reached forth into the depths of Jebediah and found the silver cord of his soul, hoping something had changed about him by now. But it was still nothing more than a razor-sharp wire, rusted and slicing into my psyche. It hurt, but I'd missed the old feeling. He groped for my spirit as well, stalking my heart, pressing into the soft spot at the back of my skull. His dissatisfaction showed through. He'd found that the well of my love for Dani was still full.

He tried to smile as if there weren't a decade of carnage between us. "Walk with me."

"All right."

Most of the tourists and spiritual seekers stayed close to Jericho Road and the Church of all Nations, facing across from the Golden Gate. They liked to look at the stone presumed to be the place where Jesus prayed before his arrest. I had no doubt that Betty Verfenstein had been here or would soon visit as part of her vacation package. Danielle would have enjoyed the serenity of the garden despite what had occurred here twenty centuries ago.

"You still love her," Jebediah said, "even after all this time—"

"Yes."

"I don't believe that someone who so desperately holds on to the past can be called a romantic. It's why you're the Lord Summoner and master of the art. This love for the dead."

I didn't argue the point. He was right, in his own fashion, and though he meant to be insulting I took a certain pride in what he said.

"Do you really want to murder more children, Jebediah?" I asked.

"Oh, don't be so tedious. They're not children. You wouldn't dare say so if you knew what viciousness they can be held accountable for. Or perhaps you would. In any case, they came to me seeking glory. Surely you, of anyone, can relate to that. Who am I to deny them the chance?"

"This absurd dream of yours isn't glorious."

He didn't hear me. His askew smile widened as he drank in the atmosphere. Swirls of remnant energy circled above us and spilled on him. "This beautiful site is known throughout the world as the place where Christ pondered his fate before the soldiers dragged him off to be executed. Do you think he kneeled there?" Jebediah pointed in one direction, then another. "Staring toward that hill? Or that promontory? Can you guess what happened in that spot centuries before Jesus stepped foot here?"

I could guess. Holy sites were usually built upon the unholy. He couldn't help feeding off the errant majiks of the land, and motes of black energy bubbled from his eyes. I didn't need to suck the marrow of massacre to know this had once been a place of child sacrifices.

I said, "Do you think a history of barbarism gives you the right to forfeit others?"

"Everyone is free to leave whenever they wish. Even you."

"If only that were true."

"It is, and always has been. We're all here of our own accord. I'm not to blame for the fate of others."

"Is that what you tell yourself when you think of Aaron?" I asked.

It stopped him cold, and the funnels of eddying power dissipated. I was glad that he cared enough to show some grief. He dropped his chin and stared thoughtfully at the ground for a minute. "I had nothing to do with that."

"Uriel's here and stands with you."

"He is my brother, after all."

"Yes, and also the murderer of your brother. You've done a hell of a job looking out for them."

That got to him. He whirled on me, the web of veins in his neck bulging. It was good to see that he could still feel so strongly about matters of family. He closed in. "They made their own choice to enter that damnable monastery. Uriel suffers for his sins, and his guilt has driven him into near-catalepsy. They each did what they believed had to be done, no different from me! Who are you to judge?"

His scars were nearly pressed against my own face as he shouted. I'd had enough of his rationalization and grabbed him by the collar. My grin was nearly as ugly as his.

The black energy encircled my eyes too, and the air burned with the stink of ozone. Sparks skittered along my new fingernails, and a hideous bark of laughter escaped me. "I watched you cut Bridgett's throat."

"She was nothing to you!"

"You refused to let my father find peace

in death and turned him into a caricature just to mock me." The rage kept surging, and a voice said, *That's it, that's it, release it all, let it go, this will be wonderful*. It wasn't Self provoking me—the voice was my own. "You set the Fetch on me and forced me to play along in your plans. You dangled my love for my lady and let the temptation drive me half mad into your trap. All of your followers lie cold in the ground, even that rag tag bunch of bitter teenagers back there. They're already dead, Jebediah, or don't you know that?"

"They do what they will!"

"Your egomania has brought you against the design of heaven, in a belief that you might raise the messiah for your own ends. You damn fool, you aren't innocent, Jebediah."

I raised my glowing fist and thought that all my pain would end now if I murdered him here without a regret.

"But you are?" he asked. And as he said it he grasped me by the back of the neck, drew me to him, and kissed me.

Perhaps all the DeLancres, even the witch killers, were equally audacious, and called to them others who were just as impudent and reckless. He shrugged, let me loose with a small and pleased laugh, and started walking off. If I'd had my athame with me I might have stuck it in his back right then, or perhaps I'd have only heard my rage, nagging me on. I grabbed him by the shoulder and spun him to face me again.

"Don't make me kill you, Jebediah. For Christ's sake—"

"Yes," he nodded. "For the sake of Christ, of course. And the world. Can't you feel the culmination of God's will approaching?"

"That's your problem. You separate large incidents from the small. Find God in the whisper."

"Like you have? You rail against him even now in your heart, for stealing your precious love. You hate and seethe with an intensity I've never seen before, and you do it under the auspices of serenity. It's sad, really."

We had walked to the limestone ridge and stared down at the narrow Kidron Valley.

"Why did you send Griffin against me?" I said.

"I didn't. He forgave you for murdering him, as I recall. I don't have the finesse to manipulate a soul as insane as that."

I believed him. "Give up this notion of resurrecting Christ."

"Can you give up your heart's desire?"

"No, not even when you turn it against me, but you're not—"

"So be it."

There was no wind.

Chapter Sixteen

Violence had flared in the Old City again. On the West Bank two Israeli soldiers had been shot, and in response several Palestinians were wounded at the Haram during a protest. There was a good deal of rock throwing and the Israelis claimed to have used rubber-coated steel pellets to disperse the crowd, but now four Palestinians were dead. Delicate peace talks had begun to break down in the wake of the latest bloodshed.

Nip sat waiting atop the Wailing Wall.

He moaned while the Jews prayed forty feet below him, writing out pleas and placing them in the cracks of the stone. Here, at least, they were all believers, though some men cursed God as they always would. I was surprised by the amount of noise and activity in the square, a vast rumble of voices and music and shouting.

Nip gave another great heaving sigh that blew knots of gray fur before his quivering nose and sent slips of paper whipping across the tiled plaza. His meaty pink paws clamped on his knees as he turned to stare down at me. I kept hoping that the spirit of Abbot John would join us. I thought I could raise him if I needed to, just so I could ask him about those dreams concerning the archangel Michael.

But I was a little afraid that after leaving the mount Abbot John's sanity had also left him, returning him to the days when he twisted the heads off dogs and raped old women in their nursing home beds. Somewhere along the line my dad's own finite rationality had been given up to him, and I dreaded what might happen if I brought it back into the world.

I gestured for Nip to come down off the wall, but he merely gazed at me. He kept lamenting and held both hands out like a child wanting to be picked up.

What's he doing?

Might be nothing. Whining is his whole gig.

Get up there and find out.

Self shot me a glare and said, *What the hell am I? A capuchin monkey? I'll fall off and break my ass!*

I took him by the neck and lifted him to the stone where the essence of God supposedly still resided. I held him to the rifts in the stone like the Jews holding their written prayers. Self hissed at me. *You've got to learn how to handle these aggressive tendencies.* I shoved and he started to scale the wall.

His claws left fresh holes in the ancient rock, as if he were purposefully scratching at the face of God. The noise escalated in the square. Everyone could feel the blasphemy occurring even if they couldn't see it, and they talked louder and read faster and sang with a note of hysteria. Rabbis glowered at me, the outsider standing alone before the Wailing Wall, neither kneeling nor weeping nor taking photos. Dust and pebbles scattered down around my feet as Self continued to climb.

When he got to the top he sat beside Nip and put his arm around the masterless familiar. Nip slumped into wild sobbing as

Self patted his back. He might mourn Uriel's treachery forever. Without his other half, Nip must have felt as empty and disconcerted as Jebediah felt without Peck in the Crown. Self pressed his face close to Nip's, and I couldn't be sure if they were speaking at all.

A hand reached out of the crowd and touched my shoulder. I spun to my left, ready for an assault from one of Jebediah's new coven members. I backed away and whispered a Mesopotamian spell, the syllables coming so easily in this land of ruthless and relentless warriors. My ears rang as Nip continued his keening moans. Hassidim pressed around, their bearded faces and muttering voices boxing me in. None of Jebediah's mad children were here, and so far as I could tell, none of the dead had come to attack. My fists began to throb with the need to kill.

At the last moment I saw the cloudy dark eyes and lengthy black hair held back in a shawl. I had to bite down hard to keep from saying the slaying curse already poised on my tongue.

It was the woman from the Chapel of the Nailed. She too had been crying. I could see that the sudden and terribly heightened sensitivity had affected her as well as everyone else in the square. A gold cross around her neck flickered in the sunlight. Hassidim scowled. She grimaced as the din increased, and though she didn't want to get too near me she was forced to so we could hear each other.

My chest tightened. This wasn't an accidental encounter. Coincidence didn't exist anymore.

Even as a Christian she'd undoubtedly visited the Temple Mount before, but it was clear she didn't enjoy being in the square, so close to the Western Wall. This was not the place for her to pray. In a city that still had quarters and remained ghettoized, the Church of the Holy Sepulcher belonged to the Christians and the Temple Mount to the Jews and the Haram to the Muslims. People died for crossing lines in the sand. It was one of the reasons why these people would never have peace.

She struggled with her decision to speak to me. Slips of paper floated down and brushed her cheek. She kept looking from side to side as if she might break into a run. I felt the same way.

She didn't want to be here, and when she peered up at me from beneath the shawl I knew she was thinking the same thing I was—that our meeting in the chapel hadn't been a fluke. Finally she said, as if still not quite believing, "My father. He told me he knows you."

"I don't know anyone in Israel."

Frustration skewered her features, and I thought she might burst into tears or give me a roundhouse to the jaw. Either was understandable, considering the situation. She looked up, wondering why the papers were falling around us.

"How did you find me?" I asked.

She frowned, thinking about it. "He told me you would be here."

In that moment she was so beautiful that I almost felt happy in a way I hadn't for ten years. I couldn't control myself and watched as I took her shawl in my hand and pulled it from her head. Her rich black hair loosened and slipped over her shoulders. Her eyes widened and so did mine. I couldn't believe I'd done that.

"I'm sorry," I said.

"It's all right." She took my arm again, squeezed once, and let go, just as she had done in the church. "My father wishes to talk to you. Please come to see him. He needs you."

"Who is your father?"

"His name is Joseph Shiya. I am Bethany. He's—"

I nodded. "Dying."

Her father was on his deathbed, and the summons of the dying held great authority and command. Her entreaty had a potency with repercussions, just as my oath on Mount Armon had.

"Yes," she said. "He is."

Again she swept aside her hair in that same gesture that made me think of Danielle. It struck such a resonant chord in me that I felt a painful heat rear in my gut. She stared at me with a puzzled expression.

I looked up and saw that Self and Nip were gone. I scanned the plaza and the Hassidim had turned back to their prayers, the near-frenzy broken.

"It's all right," I told her. "I'll come with you."

"I'm not sure that I want you to."

"I don't blame you."

"He will not even see a priest. I don't know who you are, or why he needs you so desperately."

"I'm not certain either, but your father is dying and he has something to say."

"That's true." Her gaze filled with a

swarm of confusion. They were the eyes of my mother. "Please, follow. This way."

We walked through the city, down along David Street to the Christian quarter. A couple of times I spotted Self following at a distance, weaving into alleys and shop doorways. He wasn't quite hiding but he refused to come any closer. Nip was nowhere to be seen. I wondered if this was a new game or ploy of some kind, and I didn't know what to make of it.

Bethany Shiya lived near the Jaffa Gate. The sun was setting by the time we arrived, and my raw skin had started to cool. Shadows lengthened across the wall, scrambling along the stone. I looked at the road heading toward Jaffa, leading on to the Mediterranean, and I thought of the entire world beyond. Bethany took my hand and led me on.

She ushered me up a series of steps and into her home, and I knew who her father was even before I walked into the bedroom to see him sprawled shivering beneath several blankets.

I wasn't alarmed by the pattern these circumstances had taken, but I didn't find any comfort in them either. I had told Jebediah that you could not separate large events from the small, but I found myself trying to tug at this tapestry of misfortune and miracles and hold the detached threads.

On the bed lay the man who had led me from the fire.

The ragged plowed lines of Joseph Shiya's face had deepened and darkened even more. His ashen skin looked like clay that had been pounded by an insane child. He gasped horribly for air, the wet sucking sounds filling his chest.

And yet his resolve, force of will, and beatific nature came through, even now at the hour of his death. Such sanctity made him imposing and dignified even as he dwindled to nothing. Perhaps he truly was the reincarnate of John of Patmos, who kept the Christian faith alive during its harshest years of persecution.

"It's you," he wheezed. "I'd hoped to be dead before my daughter returned with you."

So it was going to be like that.

I took a breath and swallowed down my rising irritation. "She said you asked to see me."

"And so I did."

I sat in a chair beside the bed and waited. Bethany brought me a glass of ice water. I finished it quickly and she took it from me and returned with a glass of wine. She asked if I was hungry and I thanked her but waved her off, listening to the old man's labored breathing. She closed the bedroom door and left me with him.

Death spun its gray mask over Joseph Shiya's features. His fear was palpable but I knew he wasn't scared of dying or afraid of me. This all had something to do with Bethany, and the terror enveloped him like a shroud. His shallow breath clogged in his throat with a heinous rattle.

"It's a miracle you survived the flames."

"Yes," I said.

"There were many who died."

"Yes."

"And not a mark on you."

I'd have thought that a man who wouldn't live through the night might get to the point immediately, but he felt more comfortable avoiding his dread.

"How is it you were there?" I asked.

"God is not finished with me yet."

"He never finishes with any of us."

"This is true," Joseph Shiya told me, with some steel entering his voice.

"You sound angry about it."

"Some men's destinies are larger than others," he said. "Their sacrifices greater and much uglier."

"I'm getting a little tired of all you guys telling me about my fate."

He attempted to sit up in bed but couldn't make it. I moved my chair closer and tried to help but he felt so brittle in my arms I thought he'd snap in half. His hand crept out from beneath the blankets and dropped to my leg. "Not only yours. All of us who do our duty. Men like Barrabas, Judas, and Pontius Pilate. Their lives were no less entwined than ours. Tell me, where would Christ's path have led him without these men?"

"To some place with less pain," I said.

"And what would the fate of the world have been then?"

I let loose with a weary sigh and let it just keep rolling and rolling out of me. "Did you ever consider that we all would have been a lot happier?"

"No, God surely would have destroyed us by now, but . . . but—"

Men of duty, woven into the greater scheme of God like so many thin colorful strands. Even a retarded child could play cat's cradle with a piece of yarn. There, I thought, rested the destiny of the planet.

"What did you call me here for?" I asked.

Even before the words were out of my mouth the sickness abruptly skewered through me again. I grunted and nearly fell headlong out of my seat, shaking in spasms. The wineglass tipped over and shattered. There was no lamplight in the room, and now shaggy rips of darkness appeared and widened.

The door opened and Bethany stood waiting there, staring, surprised it had been me who cried out. "Is there anything I can do?"

"No."

Self appeared behind her, slipping past her whirling skirts as she turned away. He looked feverish, as if he too were fighting the pain. Joseph Shiya seemed to sense my second self's presence and glanced about the room, searching for the approach of death. Self closed in with a buoyant step, but the old man tilted his head, listening.

" 'The day of calamity is upon the land,' " Joseph quoted from the book of Revelation. " 'The sons of light battle the company of darkness amid the clamor of gods and men.' "

It never ceased to amaze me that the Bible itself, taken as literal truth, makes so many references to there being more than one god.

Pretty catchy lyrics, Self said. *Put it together with a backbeat.*

Joseph Shiya perked up from his pillows. "Azreal . . . the angel Azreal comes."

"Not yet," I told him. "Why did you call me here?"

"There is evil here, now, with us."

Blow it out your ass, dude.

"It's all right, Joseph."

The old man grew more uneasy and excited until he clutched at my sleeve. "Only you can save her," he hissed at me. "I was wrong, I should not have obeyed my God. It is inhuman, what he asks. My daughter, you must save her."

"From what?" I asked.

"From you."

Sensible guy, I like the way he thinks.

"Joseph, listen to me. I swear I won't hurt her."

Self sat on the edge of the bed, sweating, holding his belly the same way I was. We both rocked a little, swaying, licking our lips. The heat was unbearable and there was no air. Streams of sweat slid down my chest. Self dug his claws into the sheets to hold himself steady, and he slowly ripped them to tatters.

"You must protect her from the evil that comes," Joseph Shiya cried, with tears flowing into the channels of his cross-thatched face. "From my sins. From my fears." He looked me in the eye, and I realized the terror he had was only for God. "I am a poor servant of the Lord."

Better than me! Self said, grinning through his discomfort.

"I have failed the trial of Job, the test of Abraham."

I grabbed hold of the front of the man's bedclothes and shouted, "What did you do?"

"Save her, I beg you. God forgive my unworthy soul. She rides the Dragon!"

A door had been opened in heaven.

Self leaped onto my chest and nuzzled my neck, suddenly yelping and moaning and trying to turn away, but there was nowhere to hide from this. I heard distant trumpets and a vision unfolded of locusts with men's faces carrying out their hideous duties at the apocalypse. I whispered a word but did not know it. I said it again and still, for this moment, it had no shape or meaning. I stumbled out of the room, panting heavily, the agony inside me becoming something else.

And I knew what Joseph Shiya had done. Duty calls for dedication, loss, and forfeit. What the Lord God wills must be carried out by his servants, faithfully and without question. Such devotion had cost Lot his wife, Samson his eyes, Jacob his brother, John the Baptist his head—and Christ his life.

Joseph Shiya once possessed the raw fanaticism of men like Isaac, John of Patmos, and Jebediah DeLancre. He had not failed the tests and trials set before him. Angels would praise his name, and he would be blessed in the Book of Judgment. He'd given all that he had to give, as the Lord commanded.

When his God had asked him to sacrifice his daughter, Joseph turned his back too late.

Bethany was there on her bed, naked and giggling, slithery with the sheen of her own craving and desire.

Damn, she's fine, Self whispered, dropping from my shoulder. His lusts or mine carried him forward. Ribbons of saliva dripped over his fangs.

Tom Piccirilli

My mouth had gone dry and I could barely ask, "Who are you?"

"All that you want," she said.

"What is your name?"

"I have none."

The vertigo struck again and I toppled toward the bed, even as Self fell beside me, grimacing and whimpering and chortling. She peeled my clothes from me as my second self rolled at the foot of the bed. Her lips went to my chest and something broke deep inside me and I tried to yell, but all that came out was a groan of pleasure. It had been so long. I held my hands around her throat but I couldn't tighten them. There are dreams you never awaken from. They are as much a part of you now as ever, alive beneath your civilized skin and pretenses at humanity. I laughed, loud and revolting, drawing Bethany to me. Self licked her neck and she purred.

My love and loyalty to Danielle had remained my one pure accomplishment, and now, as I sank into this mad bliss, even that was gone.

Of red bellies and ripped knees, the taste of pale—

I couldn't do anything but exactly what Bethany wanted, except that she was no

290

longer any Bethany. The great whore whom we've all fornicated with consumed her and consumed me. Babylon the Great, mother of harlots and abominations.

The word I had spoken was whore.

Joseph Shiya continued to rant in the other room, muttering and crying. His voice was already full of gravel from the bottom of his own grave. "I can hear them! The seven angels blowing the seven trumpets! He comes, the lamb with seven horns and seven eyes. The spirit of God has released the pale horse."

"Shut up!" I shouted.

"There shall be a hail of fire and blood, stars will go out and fall! The locusts shall be set free to torment the faithless, wearing breastplates, with tails like scorpions and faces of men." His death rattle went on and on. "And there, finally, Azreal is hovering in the corner. I die, I die! Forgive me my weaknesses, oh Lord, I beg you, do not forsake me at this hour—"

I fell onto Bethany again and her teeth sank into my shoulder. Self left long bloody welts along her thighs and back and she moaned for more. My new flesh sizzled worse than when I'd roasted in the fire. I could feel the thrust of her laughter against my throat. Self slipped between us, weaving, there and not there as his own desires moved him. I didn't know who was touching her anymore, him or me. He wagged his trembling ass, bursting with need and joy. She struck me and I dropped onto her with my fists and tongue.

Her hair draped across my belly and didn't stop. It continued falling across me and my entire life: drenched, womanly, warm, and soft. The blackness was the very depth of my fears and wants, as she brushed me again. She tossed her hair in that practiced manner reminiscent of my lost love. It was I who had failed the test and willingly entered the tender ambush.

Bethany encompassed us both. "See the smoke of my burning," she said. "Wail for me."

I did.

Lord, I did, as we were all devoured by the endlessly heaving, sweet oblivion.

When I woke in the morning I was already weeping.

It was the day before Easter. Bethany lay on the bed. Her belly was red and her knees had been torn. She was unlike the woman who had bedded me last night because she did not rouse or smile or chew.

Self sat in her viscera and screeched, *Don't look at me!*

I tried not to.

Instead, I stared at what was left of Bethany, lying unwrapped on the sheets and splayed across the floor.

My name had been carved into her chest, and I was covered in blood.

Chapter Seventeen

The raging clashes continued to escalate. Israeli troops battled several gunmen and thousands of rock-throwing Palestinians. They opened fire on the rioters, killing twelve and wounding hundreds. The bloody confrontations in the West Bank and Gaza Strip would only grow worse as activists and followers marched on Israeli army positions. Thousands of protesters chanted the Muslim battle cry "Allahu Ak-bar."

God is great.

Streets became littered with rocks and overturned garbage bins while plumes of smoke from blazing tires rose into the sky.

Police were forced to evacuate tourists off the streets of the Old City. Palestinian youths hurled stones, some twirling slingshots for a longer aim. They set fire to the Israeli police station at the Lion's Gate entrance during an attempt to take it over. Many carried black flags of mourning for those killed. Others stuffed gas-soaked rags into bottles and threw them at Israeli soldiers, who fired rubber-coated steel pellets and live rounds from behind walls. Gunmen, their faces covered by checkered head scarves and ski masks, shot at troops crouching behind jeeps in protracted firefights.

In the heart of the desert, it began to hail.

Fragments of ice had flecks of frozen blood in them. The air had started to spasm, as if the lack of motion and its very staleness were causing it to somehow convulse. The day grew dark, but not with clouds—frigid sunlight still shined but the world simply became blacker.

What did you do to me?

What?

You healed my body but you changed me. What did you let loose?

Self stared at me sadly. *You've changed me,* he said.

Did you do it?

Do what?

The girl . . .

Do what!

I drew him to me until our noses touched. *Did you kill the girl?*

He yanked on my shirt until his claws dug into my neck and blood welled. *Did you? Tell me! Did you?*

Which side are you on?

On your side, like always. Then he frowned so hard that the ridge appeared between his eyes, as it did between mine, both of us looking genuinely confused. *But which side are you on? Do you even know?*

The land itself had grown hostile with resentment. I sat in front of a church for hours, and then moved off to a mosque and a Muslim shrine and I watched the different flags droop in the unmoving air and couldn't tell them apart. I vomited in alleyways until the bile tore up my guts. Gunshots and the sound of breaking glass echoed in all directions.

Self sniffed, held his nose, and said, *You really stink*.

I lay under garbage as the hail stormed down. Even with the sunlight igniting the jewels of blood in the slivers of ice, I enjoyed the cold on my blistered and bitten skin. Helicopters passed overhead, hovering, silhouetted in the sky, hanging against the sun until it became as black as a sackcloth of hair or ashes.

Joseph and Bethany Shiya's corpses might not be found for days. The lust and illness had been purged from me in a sacrifice I did not make. The great whore that had possessed Bethany had fed well on all of us.

Why hadn't my throat been cut?

Bethany's body had been carved open in the exact same manner as Theresa Verfenstein thirty-five years ago on a New Jersey campus. Even my name had been sliced into the flesh with the same decisive, steady strokes. A right-hand curve, sloping low and dragging with a slight flourishing curl. The killer must have had some real strength in order to leave chips in the rib cage and sternum.

I'd fulfilled another prophecy out of Revelation, lying with the mother of whores. I was being used, step by step, but couldn't figure out a way to stop it.

What happened to us in there? What did you see?

I didn't see anything.

You don't sleep. You must've allowed this to happen.

I don't sleep but I'm not always awake. He scratched his cheek and peered around. *Damn, I could use a latte and some more sugar cookies. I think I'm hypoglycemic.*

A footstep sounded and a bird screeched loudly behind me.

I waited. The footsteps came closer. I could feel the anticipation pulsating all around, but it wasn't mine. Somebody else wanted a piece of me and expected this moment to be important and memorable. He twined between the shadows and finally appeared at the mouth of the alley, where he found me huddled under the strewn rubbish facedown in the street.

That was all right. Situations like this could no longer shame me.

His bird tilted its head and whispered in his ear. He nodded and took a step closer, unafraid and indiscreet.

I stared at him for a minute and still couldn't really distinguish him from the rest of the coven. He stood tall, six-three, and had an oily smile that kept his lips sliding. A loosely curled shock of hair hung off his forehead, the kind that girls would love to catch in their fingers and play with for hours. He looked as though he should be in some college English lit program, leaning back in his seat, intense but casual, that greasy grin oozing as he argued with his professor about the subtext metaphor and vagaries of Voltaire's *Candide*.

Twenty-one or twenty-two, maybe, and he'd been killing them for years.

He was another necromancer, somebody in love with the dead. I didn't need to deal with any more trouble today. His eyes gleamed with a heady brew of humor and maleficia. He had beauty and charm and had used them in vile ways. Ghosts clung to him by the dozens—middle-aged women he'd drawn to him with his smile.

"What's your name?" I asked.

The jackdaw Hotfoot Johnson whispered to the kid again, like some lawyer clearing all his answers. "Marcus," he said.

"What do you want, Marcus?"

"To learn from you."

It didn't seem incongruous to either of us that we spoke amongst trash, with the bloody hail coming down. "No," I told him. "Now leave."

"I can't do that."

"Why? Are you under orders to stick close in case I don't plan on showing tomorrow?"

"No, nothing like that. We all know you'll help Jebediah."

"Really."

"Yes, or else why would you be here? You rely too much upon each other. You're the Lord Summoner."

It was true, but that didn't have to mean anything to me. I held my fist open and stared at my variant lifeline again. I wanted it moved back to where it belonged. In which one of my lives had I been safer, and saner?

"I turn the title over to you, kid."

The fluid grin flowed and dipped and finally settled. "What?"

"You heard me. You're boss hog around here now. You can start by bringing back all these ladies you've murdered."

He actually let out a chuckle, and his bottom lip jutted. Some of the dead women wafted closer to him, still wanting to nibble at his boyish pout. He said, "I didn't hurt anyone."

Marcus had a natural talent for sifting through facts and feelings, inspecting each and moving on. I could understand why the women stayed with him. I looked closer and saw that most of them were suicides—the skin flaps and razor gashes trailed up their forearms. No hesitation cuts at all. They couldn't live without him when he left.

"They died because of you."

"We all die because of someone else."

"You might be right."

He had a haughty attitude, like most of the pretentious witches I'd known. He found great calm in certain atrocities, and that intrigued me.

Squatting in the trash he said, "You're foolish for having left him. With your knowledge and skill at the craft you could have had anything you desired—"

"Is that right?"

"—but you left. Why?"

"Get out of here."

"Why did you give up everything for one insignificant woman? Her death was a blessing according to Jebediah, and instead of appreciating it you've wasted a lifetime of power in order to . . ."

I stood and punched him in the jaw.

It barely connected. The jackdaw screeched and flew in circles overhead. Marcus had speed and dexterity and instead of going over backward and hitting the street hard he just sort of glided away. Any other time it would have worked fine, but he slipped on the bleeding ice and went down anyway. It seemed to amuse him and he let loose with a quiet titter.

He ran it out for a couple of seconds, and then with a serious edge he said, "I'm sorry I offended you. Jebediah said—"

"Jebediah lies, but you'll find that out soon enough."

"Everyone lies."

Hotfoot Johnson eyed Self and thrust its open beak at us. We were only ten feet apart. Self crooked his finger and beckoned the bird forward. The jackdaw unfurled its wings, hissed a particularly nasty curse, and came soaring for my eyes. Even Marcus seemed shocked that his familiar would attack.

Self launched himself forward as the blackbird approached. Marcus shouted and reached way too late. Hotfoot Johnson came at me with its tongue hanging, each feather angled like a saber. There wasn't any time for me to move as it covered the space between us at an amazing speed, those talons glittering with ice as they spread now to impale me.

Self took the bird in flight a few inches from my face and wrestled it to the ground in a cloud of feathers.

Any trouble? I asked.

Not for me.

Marcus wasn't torn by loyalty. He hardly even looked at his squawking familiar being almost crushed in the street. The kid had determination and will but could cast aside his other self in the same fashion he threw off his lovers. I wanted to see what he had inside.

While he sat there rubbing his chin I reached out and clipped the women from him. Not all of them would leave Marcus even when they were free to go on. Several stayed wafting about him, still in love, decaying but no longer lonely.

"Did you think they all hated me?" he asked.

"No, I don't suppose I did."

You couldn't even guess at the dealings of the human heart.

In the back of my mind I could hear the slow, grating chant of his consciousness probing for my secrets. It was a subtle and rather dainty touch, more of a caress designed to impress a forlorn woman riding the crest of middle age.

"You really want into my head?" I asked.

"Yes," Marcus said. The agitated smile quivered and danced all over the place.

"Okay. Start the dance."

That sluggish chanting continued as he gathered himself—he had no agenda other than to learn by stealing my hard-earned knowledge. That just wasn't the way it was done. Maybe it even would have been funny if we weren't perched at the apocalypse.

Self said, *Quit playing and lay this little creep to waste.*

I kind of like him.

No, you don't.

I could feel my past loosening and rising in me once again, floating to the surface from the bottomless mire of my own forgotten myths. Marcus did not think of God or vision. He didn't even care for the ladies anymore, or his brood. He had something he wanted more desperately than his own soul, and he wouldn't stop until he got it. I'd been there once myself and knew it would only lead to a route of bliss, treachery, and heartbreak. If this kid wasn't already going to fry in hell, he would've been headed there now on a bullet train, embracing each flame in perfect passion.

Marcus's eyes went from pale blue to septic yellow, narrowing in triumph as he swam in the murky depths of my soul.

The hail in our hair slowly melted and left

sprinkles of blood on our faces and clothes. He loved the dead and he even loved my dead. His psychic manipulation grew stronger, the spike piercing as he dug in and rutted around. His will parted the layers of my guilt and panic and anguish, pressing deeper but without any pain. He had the touch, I had to give him that. He flipped the pages of every book he found in all the many rooms of my mind. Snatches of songs and the grumbling of my first car's engine made him turn and wander through garages and backyards, watching the church tower and the insane asylum in the distance. He read the names off headstones and pressed his finger into the chiseled letters, feeling the near-electrical smoothness of the polished stone. The kid knew his way around a charnel house of the heart, stroking the drenched walls and stained floors of my life.

Danielle was first on the slab, lying directly beside my mother. They lay dressed in white, absolutely pure and lovely even while surrounded by the bone dust and rusted blades. He picked up scraps of my past from the tables and shelves: candles and chalk, grimoires, mason jars, gris-gris pouches, solar wheels, amulets, the fat fingers of a thief turned into a hand of glory, knotted aguilette cords, my athame, and all the substance and material of our kind. The salamanders ran past his feet throwing fire, but nothing ever burned here.

He walked among rows and rows of the slain, peeking under sheets and trying to commit faces to memory, but they kept changing even as he stared. That always happened. They all became Danielle or my mother.

Marcus's smile finally stopped squirming. "They're so beautiful."

"Yes," I told him, "they are."

"And you did this?"

"More or less."

He bent forward to brush his lips against the cheek of my lost love. He tilted his head back and enjoyed her fragrance, letting a small laugh roll in the back of his throat before stooping over her again. He sniffed softly, murmuring words of tenderness and devotion as the tip of his tongue jutted to take a taste of flesh, and Danielle's eyes opened.

She grinned a mouthful of blood and reached out with animal swiftness, not quite cackling but, Christ, it was close, hugging him to her, despising. My mother rose from a dozen different directions and immediately flung herself onto his back, screaming out my failures and crimes. Then more of the dead broke free from the darkness, overturning furniture and knocking aside the shelves of books and diagrams. My obliterated coven crept from each corner as Marcus cried out and tried to run. They each grabbed a piece of him and held on, as they did to me and forever would, nails and teeth like barbs twisting deep into muscles and tendons. Danielle pointed, accusing as she always did in my nightmares—those long thin fingers stretching, denouncing me or only reaching out for help—hyperextended as the joints in her fingers popped one after the other, elbow and wrist cracking, and still she pointed at my heart.

Marcus kept struggling to get out, trying to escape from something that can never be escaped. It wasn't until he spun completely around now that he saw I'd closed and barred the charnel house door. His jaw dropped to his chest when he realized he was trapped.

"No," he groaned as they covered him, writhing and punishing. "You can't . . . wait . . . !"

Hotfoot Johnson fought to get free as Marcus tottered a few steps in the street, gurgling like an irritated baby. He finally managed to gulp enough air to let out a scream. It came from the recesses of his soul, and when it finally ran out he kept shrieking without sound. His mouth opened wider and wider until I could hear the hinges of his jaw creaking, but still nothing came out. His women twirled about him, hugging and tugging at his wrists.

He seized his head with both hands, trying to squeeze my fear and faults out of his brain, just as someone came up from behind and brought a stick down on the back of his skull.

Marcus floundered and dropped onto his face, rolled over twice, and lay still. The jackdaw broke from Self's grip and flew to its master, where it sat on his chest making weeping sounds.

Fane drifted from the shadows, his bloodshot eyes appearing more tired than bitter. He stood holding one of his pine splints in his fist. It was too light and thin to have actually hurt Marcus if the kid hadn't already been collapsing.

I could tell that Fane badly missed his

robes, scapular, tunic, and cowl. He wore a black wrap usually seen only on Muslim women. The scent of heavy oils and pine preceded him by twenty feet as he limped toward me.

"You could've beaten that boy easily," he said. "Why didn't you?"

"Don't ask questions you don't want to know the answers to, Fane, or I'll let you inside my head too."

He was smart enough to be scared by that.

The distant noise of a Harley back-ending a flatbed trailer and the shrieks and breaking glass followed as we turned and walked out of the alley. Man, did that get old fast. I wondered if it made him a better or worse penitent for having been dead on the operating table those twelve minutes after his accident. His victims didn't trail him, so perhaps he had found some redemption in purgatory.

"I've been to the Givat Ram campus of Hebrew University," he said, "and I spent time at the Shrine of the Book to look at the Dead Sea Scrolls. I spent much of the morning at the Yad Vashem Holocaust memorial."

"You're a regular tourist."

"They're evacuating visitors. You can feel the city about to tear itself to shreds, but I needed to stay."

"Why?" I asked.

He still drew strength from the weakness in his legs, hobbling fast to keep up the pace and enjoying the agony it brought. "I wanted to see and learn all I could while I was here in the Holy Land. My intent was to discover something that might help."

"Did you find out anything useful?"

"No," he said while the motorcycle trapped in his former life echoed behind us. I thought perhaps he'd found God again, but not yet his soul. Maybe there was still time. "Nothing that might help in the coming battle." He rankled his nose at me. "You need a bath."

"I've had a bad day."

He nodded at that and we didn't say anything for a time as we walked. The hail had ended. Self glanced about moodily, and once I caught him looking into his own palm. I stopped at a shop and got him some cookies, which he ate noisily. He offered one to Fane, and Fane took it and held on to it but didn't take a bite. He said, "I was visited by John this morning."

That stopped me. "In a dream?"

"I don't really know. Possibly. I felt awake and I was standing, but I often am in my dreams."

Fane had plenty of his own Freudian traumas to deal with, and I couldn't be certain if the abbot had returned or if Fane's subconscious was merely boiling over with hidden meaning.

"What did he say?"

"He said that the first angel has been loosed. The other six will soon follow. And Michael remains chained."

Several hundred Jewish settlers attacked Israeli Arabs' homes in Nazareth. Sporadic conflicts and further rioting spilled into Hebron, Bidiya Village, Jisr al-Zarka, Netzarim Junction, and the Erez border crossing. Israelis took to the streets in anti-Arab protests at several points throughout the country. In northern Israel, at Tiberias, residents raised an Israeli flag over a mosque and set fire to the building before police restored order.

The full moon rose over Babylon.

I made it back to the gratis hotel room and could feel the presence of my mother as I walked the corridors. I knew someone was already in my room.

I turned on the light.

My father sat on the edge of the bed and stared blankly ahead.

Gawain lay on the floor, hands folded neatly over his belly. His blind eyes focused on me and the corners of his mouth lifted. He'd been stabbed twice in the stomach.

I kneeled beside him and took his head in my lap. I tried to make him as comfortable as possible. He did not appear to be in pain. His serpent's tongue twined as he mouthed words I didn't understand. I talked to him for a few minutes about nothing that mattered as my tears trickled onto his forehead. He closed his eyes and let out his last breath.

We stayed like that for an hour while I cradled Gawain's corpse, and finally I accepted that this truly was the apocalypse.

Self crouched at the window and pointed into the sky as the bloated moon slowly became as blood.

Finally my dad turned and looked at me. With that mad intelligence blazing in his moronic gaze he whispered, "Megiddo."

Chapter Eighteen

It was Easter Sunday.

Most of the train and bus service had been disrupted due to the disorder. I decided to rent a car from Sixt on King David Street. They were reluctant to let me have the Jaguar XJ8, but I paid in cash and took all the insurance.

If we were going to travel to the end of the world, then we might as well cruise there in style.

It was dangerous to be out. The heavy hail came down in fits and starts. Israeli helicopter gunships kept up their buzzing and Palestinians were lynching and setting fire to anyone they considered an Israeli spy.

Mobs roamed freely. The drive to Megiddo would take us through some of the worst areas of the fighting. It would keep everything in context, listening to the shouts and shrieks in these days of rage.

I was eager to get started. I'd never owned a car that came close to the roaring power, stealth, and deftness of the Jag. Who would have guessed you could get such a quality beast here in the Middle East, at the brink of the final war, while children huddled against stone walls and had their kidneys shot out, on the day Christ had risen two thousand years ago?

My father sat in the backseat with Self, and they held hands like a parent and child. They whispered together and occasionally tittered. Self complained about his hypoglycemia some more so I stopped at a bakery and got him a hazelnut honey lekach.

He took two bites out of it and spat it on the ground. *Gross! There's ginger in this!*

Hey!

And nutmeg! Go get me some challah bread!

You ungrateful little bastard!

He went around spitting like a cat. *You couldn't just get a slice of apple pie? A few cupcakes or hamantashen?* A growl emerged from the back of his throat. *Can't you ever do anything right?*

Who the hell do you think you are?

I know who I am in hell. Who are you?

I drew my hand back knowing what I was about to do but not completely sure why I was doing it. As if from a great distance I watched as my palm came down and struck Self across his cheek. It startled him enough to make him go *Wha!* He blinked twice. His bottom lip quivered and then he leaped.

He climbed my shirt and grabbed me by the collar, panting in my face. *You aren't going to make it.*

Then you won't either.

You're wrong. I'll never die.

Get in the car.

I need sugar! I feel light-headed!

Come on! Let's go.

He jumped down and got back into the Jag and thrashed around in the seat for a few minutes as we drove. Soon, my father began making faces against the window, yanking his mouth wide with his pinkies and mashing his nose on the glass. After a while Self did the same and they laughed until they could hardly breathe.

I was losing control. I started having

memory flashes of the times when my dad had taught me to swim in our pool and taken me to the beach. They became so strong that after twenty minutes I had to pull over because my hands were trembling so badly. I flung open the door and listened to the shouts of thousands. Neither of them got out of the car while I staggered around in the dust.

I couldn't shake my thoughts and kept remembering when my father used to drive us to the shore. How we'd walk down the dunes and see the damaged remnants of cyclone fencing. He'd hike me to his shoulder and carry me past the goldfish pond, the ice cream stands along the boardwalk, and all the pockets of pale short-tempered people with their stinking sunscreen and umbrellas positioned as if to stop a stampede. When he put me down in the water it would only take a minute before the waves and wet sucking sand had buried our feet. I'd take a stance behind him and watch as the roiling surf and foam broke against his heavily muscled legs.

I could smell other Easters, the chocolate bunnies and spring in the park. My mother's dresses were always dappled with flour or honey, but her cakes never quite

A Lower Deep

rose enough and were always burned black around the edges. The sun sifted in over her shoulder as she turned, one hand on her hip, the other smoothing back a tangle of her hair, with the fiery light enveloping each angle of her face and catching in the beads of sweat flecking the point of her chin. Dad would rush into the kitchen like a bursting storm, sometimes smiling as he knotted his tie, sometimes upset with his lips smashed white, in the years after we were no longer allowed to attend church.

I walked back to the Jag and leaned against the car door with my hands on the hood. I crouched, looked inside, and said, "Dad, tell me . . . do you know where Michael is?"

The changing of our roles was as common as it was profound. All men grow and watch their fathers weaken from legends into old men. All men bury their fathers.

He crooked his finger and beckoned me to him.

I held my face up to his with the window between us, and in a way I'd never felt closer to him.

He stuck his black tongue out and said, "Woo woo."

My hair was thick with ice crystals, and

319

when I moved my curls rang together in harmony with my father's jangling. I had a flash of déjà vu. This had happened before at the mount. We hadn't gone anywhere, he and I. Despite these trials and all this damnation over the years, we were in pretty much the same place we'd started out, vying for who might be the bigger fool. At least he was finally having some fun now.

When I got back in, Self started singing from "The Wizard of Oz" and Dad went along with it, swaying in his seat as if it were a jazz blues riff and he was grooving back in his beatnik days. *We're off to see the Wizard . . .*

Coming over a hill I saw Fane hobbling down the road. I considered just tapping the horn and passing him, but I couldn't be bothered with such spite. I pulled up alongside and said, "Hop in."

I could tell he wanted to walk the distance. That fanatic enthusiasm of the martyr was bright in his eyes from all the glorious discomfort he was in. He'd been walking for hours and would've crawled if he'd had to. Letting me drive him to the apocalypse in an air-conditioned Jaguar wouldn't count for as great sacrifice in the Book of Judgment, but Fane didn't want to miss out on the battle. He stumbled around to the passenger side and got in. "Thank you."

"Don't mention it."

Nip had been leading Fane by about fifty yards, as if ashamed to be seen with him. I pulled up and Nip got in the backseat too, still weeping and groaning as my father swayed to his own rhythms and Self went into another chorus. *Because of the wonderful things he does . . .*

"You're making a joke of this," Fane said to me.

"You think so, huh?"

"Yes."

I glanced over and wondered if Fane would have enjoyed having both his arms broken nearly as much as he did his crooked, pitiful legs.

"Listen," I said, and my voice was already quaking. "Yesterday morning I woke up lying beside a butchered woman who'd been taken over by the mother of all harlots and—"

"Another prophecy fulfilled."

"Don't interrupt me, Fane! Last night Gawain bled to death in my arms. Now I'm going to Har Meggidon to face a man I once loved above any other, who tells me if I help him bring our messiah back he'll return to me the woman who made my life worth living. It almost sounds funny, doesn't it?" I glared at Fane and squeezed the wheel until the steering column began to groan. "I've got a fair amount on my mind right now, so don't give me any shit. I didn't have to make this a game. It was a hoax long before I ever got into it."

"Your self-pity is evident," he said.

You talkin' to me? Self's DeNiro still needed work

"Yeah, well, sorry," I hissed at Fane, "but I'm in something of a mood."

"You've never learned the worth of servitude."

"Yes, I have. It's worth nothing. If you weren't always squirming in your own torment you'd know that."

He sighed and shook his head, and I thought he might actually smile. "Each of us enjoys our own agony too much."

"Yes," I said. The air conditioner circulated his noxious perfumes and I had to turn the vents in his direction. "It's the devil, you know."

"You blaspheme even now."

"Especially now, wouldn't you say? The Holy Land is brimming in the blood of children and suicidal believers, but they're not dying with the love of God in their hearts."

"You don't know that."

"I do know that. They're only seething, and they'll keep up their frenzy until they all spill apart in the dust."

It was nothing compared to the coming days, when heaven and hell burst wide open as the wars began, and the stars fell into the boiling oceans and earth became a poisoned cinder.

Are we almost there yet? Self asked.

The street was empty but there'd been fighting here recently, with burned-out trucks littering the walkways. I hit a pothole two feet deep and Fane blanched and let out a gasp as his mangled knees clacked together. He spoke through his gritted teeth. "A third of the earth's population will begin dying soon. Today is the start of a war between the sons of light and the sons of darkness. Tell me where you'll stand."

"I'll let you know when the time comes."

"You're not even sure, are you?"

My father let out a knowing high-pitched giggle that made me want to scream. "Well, if you don't like the answer you can always slap me around with your pine sticks."

Fane drew his stiletto and scraped the

edge of the blade against the underside of his chin. It might have been a threat of murder or suicide. "Something like that."

Floor this bitch! Self shouted, and I did.

And so we came to the Plain of Esdraelon in the Jezreel Valley, just west of the Jordan River, and faced the entrance to Tel Megiddo.

In the distance we could see Mount Tabor to the northeast and Mount Gilboa to the south. The watercourse of the Kishon River kept the soil productive as an agricultural region. There were crops of wheat, corn, and cotton, and my dad went into a sneezing fit because of the heavy odor from the tobacco fields.

Megiddo, the place of battles, connected all the cities of the ancient world. To control it was to control trade and the movement of armies from the pyramids to Babylon and Mesopotamia. It had once been the most heavily fortified city in Israel while the first straw huts were being built in a village that would become Rome and one day conquer all of the Holy Land.

I could feel the death of millions in the air. We all could. Over the millennia more than twenty-five cities had been built and destroyed on this same spot, one on top of the other, erected on a foundation of obliterated armies. The surrounding land was fertile with bonemeal. No wonder they believed this was where the final conflict would take place. All major wars of the ancient Middle East had centered directly on this spot.

Here too the Israelites worshipped Baal, and the archeological vestiges of altars and pillars still existed where the child sacrifices took place.

Not even a brownie, Self whined. *You couldn't get me a brownie? My blood pressure is low!*

I parked the Jag and we all got out except for Nip. He just sat there in the backseat with the tears coursing through his fur. He didn't want to take the chance of seeing disloyal Uriel again, so I left him there.

Fane limped alongside me through the ruins and said, "I can hear that jackdaw."

"They're all here," I told him. "I feel Elijah's hatred too."

"Within the Nephilim?"

"I suppose so, unless he abandoned the body."

"And what of Michael?"

"Yeah," I said, "and what about Michael?"

Fane gulped air and said, "I hope you make the right choice today."

"I thought you trusted me because I had nothing to lose or gain. I thought you pitied me."

"I don't pity you that much."

"Well, don't be shy. If you know the right way to follow God's will, you just let me know."

He stuck out his hand and it took me a second to realize he wanted me to shake with him. "Peace be with you."

I shook with him. "Sure, same to you."

We moved through the remnants of an annihilated city following the incessant screeching of Hotfoot Johnson, the squealing and mewling of the other familiars, and the overwhelming weight of consequence. My father no longer laughed aloud but he continued smiling inanely. If I had one great regret outside of the night Dani died, it was that I couldn't remove that goddamn clown costume from him.

Self touched one of the crumbling stone altars and said, *Baal got fed a lot of kiddies here.*

Yes.

If he didn't get his supper he would have torn out their eyes, and they knew it. He would've dug their smallest veins out inch by inch and knotted their unraveled intestines together.

Listen, do you always have to—

Those old-time Israelites didn't mind feeding him. Oh no!

Don't you think we ought to be a little more focused?

But some of us need to beg just to get a friggin' piece of cake!

My hand had been hurting ever since I'd struck him, and now the pain grew so bad I couldn't ignore it any longer. I looked into my palm and saw my lifeline changing again even as I watched. It crawled and shifted from one pattern into another. Perhaps I still had a few choices left.

We stepped from between two pillars and once again I stood before my coven.

There are meetings you never think about or dream of but you expect nonetheless. There was no surprise in any of our faces. Perhaps I had simply been fighting an unalterable fate as they'd been telling me the whole time. Maybe I hadn't been led here at all but had instead led each one of the others.

I walked to them slowly, casually, as if returning home. Perhaps I was, in a fashion.

Jebediah appeared dangerous, assertive, moderately aggressive, and a little bit crazy. I saw through the gossamer act and knew he was both anxious and frightened. His face crumpled in on itself until he had the expression of a sixteen-year-old boy about to get laid for the first time.

Somewhere along the line this had stopped being his plan and had spiraled out of his limited control. He was draped in the white robes of a coven leader, the same ones he had worn the night of our final sabbat. I fingered the cloth—it had been rethreaded and rewoven but I could still see the vestiges of stains and burns.

"Rejoice," he said.

"Oh, shut the hell up."

His scars seemed to ripple as he smirked. "We stand at the dawn of a new age. Be proud. Put your old angers and malice away. Every wound is about to be healed."

"Tell me," I said, "are you doing this because you want to remember your past or because you want to forget it?"

He moved in close as if to kiss me again. "The same as you," he said and left it at that.

"You really are an asshole."

"The mystery of God is finished," he said.

The ten kids of his new flock were panicky but quiet, constantly looking toward Jebediah for reassurance. Good luck, I thought, there's not much chance you'll find it there. Uriel had cut off a few more of his knuckles but he still had enough fingers to hold Aaron's sword. He carried the blade in the crook of his arm, pointed straight up like a solider about to present arms.

Among the coven again, Marcus fell back into anonymity. It took me a minute to find him among the other young men with similar features and equally disturbed penetrating eyes. He had his sleek grin back but it was only stale bravado. I could see his fear and he could see mine, and I really wished he'd just get away from here. I wished they'd all get away from here.

"How about if you send all these people back home and you and I finish this thing alone?"

"I would if you really meant it," Jebediah said.

There hadn't been any anger in me for a while—not even when I'd trapped Marcus or held Gawain dying in my arms. Only when I'd slapped Self, and that was significant. Perhaps all our wounds really were about to be healed, in one way or another.

The two girls impregnated by Fuceas appeared ready to burst, and I could tell that bothered Jebediah. The introduction of other participants would alter the plan he'd worked so hard to achieve, even as he watched it already changing and slipping further away from him.

This place and these people were as familiar to me as a recurring nightmare.

My father hovered about a dozen feet away, dancing and clapping alone like a child making his own fun.

The coven enjoyed the gathering of forces. It was their first real taste of the enormity of time, vision, and dream that they'd tasted. They'd fashioned themselves into a circle of power, taking their rightful places. Jebediah had trained them well, and they each moved fluidly with a perfect syncopation. Marcus kept his eyes on mine, maybe wanting to kill me or only earn my respect. If anybody got out of this alive, I was sure it would be he.

I'd allowed him to run loose inside my head and he'd learned from it. He had a new element to his nature now, a respect for the sacrifices that had to be made. His women sought his attention but he ignored them, concentrating, wary. He'd brushed up against my soul and some of my past clung to him like paint. He had other shades swirling around him, just the barest wisps that Hotfoot Johnson tried to stab at with its beak. Marcus would be haunted with a touch of guilt for the rest of his life, my guilt if not his own. Danielle and my mother had become his ghosts as well.

"It's not too late, Jebediah," I said.

"It's always been too late for us. Sometimes I think this was the only reason I was ever born"—he turned and the immense sadness in his eyes made me want to hold him tightly, the way I once had—"just to bring you here on this day, at this hour."

"We don't need to do this."

"Of course we do. We're no less God's slaves as the Seraphim or Satan or the rabbis or Christ Himself. Our lives were written out the moment God became aware and separated light from darkness."

"You can't really believe that," I said, although it was a thought I'd had on more than one occasion myself.

"Perhaps I do." Then he shrugged. "Perhaps not. We'll be beginning soon. Prepare and ready yourself."

"I am."

"I know, you're always ready to raise the dead. It's your beautiful genius."

I expected him to walk away but he didn't. He stood at my side and looked out over the Jezreel Valley and I could see the pulse in his neck hammering so quickly that I thought he might have a heart attack any second now. Sweat poured off my face. Elijah's fury washed against me like blasts of steam, but I still couldn't see the giant Nephilim anywhere. Elijah had either left the hybrid body or changed it or was still on his way here with his hatred leading him by miles.

Fane took up position near Uriel and tried speaking to him but got no response. Self found the spirit of Bridgett floating about and started getting funky with her again, climbing and clawing. The flaps of her slashed throat slapped together loudly and sent echoes across the plain.

The sound of mutilated flesh excited the other familiars. There was a sudden din of their hungry and lustful cries and titters. Jamara the fat legless spaniel slid itself toward Bridgett in the hopes of stuffing its tongue into the gaping wound of her ghost. His mother Thummin was nowhere to be seen. Vinegar Robyn and Mr. Broadeye Sack, and the black owl Prickeare started slinking around, edging toward Bridgett's stink of church. Self had to slap them away.

I'd almost forgotten why we were doing this. It took me a while to remember that Jebediah had said we could force our way into paradise and sit at God's left hand. I didn't know why we'd want to.

That yellow cracked tooth crept out from under his shredded lip and glinted at me. "We've come full circle."

"Stop saying that." It might have been the truth, but I didn't need to be constantly reminded of the fact.

"We need blood."

"Considering how many of your flock have already been murdered, I'd say maybe you had your own preoccupation and love for the dead."

"Assuredly. I need their aid from the other side, to bring Christ closer to us."

It didn't take long before he was back in form. The sorrow in his face fled and the fiery madness slid back into place. I thought his own lifeline might be skittering around in his hand and driving him even more crazy. I could tell that he suddenly wanted to kill someone, and his eyes settled on Uriel. He wanted to murder his brother for revenge as much as to put Uriel out of his own pointless misery. Chop him down to pieces, inch by inch, just as he'd done himself. Perhaps Uriel would even help.

"We need blood," he repeated, almost pleasantly, smiling, and taking a step toward his brother.

I grabbed Jebediah's shoulder. "There's already enough death here and has been for five thousand years. Where's Elijah?"

"What?"

"Where's Elijah?"

I thought that might make him drop his smile, and it did. The Nephilim was another variable that might disrupt his bizarre plans if he actually had any, and I was no longer sure that he did. "Coming."

Chapter Nineteen

Jebediah used his athame to mark the circle of power in the dirt, eighteen feet in diameter, as he walked deosil—clockwise—in association with the course of the sun and stars. The other coven members took their places in a circle. Each of the four cardinal points were covered exactly, with me and Jebediah standing to the north, associated with earth, the pentacle, secrecy, and the color black. This purified space acted as a boundary for the reservoir of our concentrated will.

We made the correct cleansing gestures and began chanting, each word and phrase awakening emotions, memories, and visualizations of energies and eons. I could make out a faint silvery glow about each of us. Sparks began to bounce around the ruins as if the swords of the slain warring soldiers still clashed together.

The darkened sun loomed over us. The girls carrying the offspring of Fuceas could barely stand, and I imagined the yolk of the demon earl eating them from the inside out, ready to spring to life. The spirits of Janus and Rachel swam over them, jealous that their own profane children had never come full term and been born into the human world.

My father stood beside me, wandering to the edge of the majik circle, dancing along its edge and then stepping back. Self leaped to Dad and sat atop his shoulder the way I once did as a child.

Hey, mon, we should be on de island of sunshine and plenty, not here.

You sure about that?

This is bad juju, I'd know that even if I wasn't starving.

We get out of this one and I'll set you up with a lifetime supply of glazed doughnuts.

With chocolate sprinkles?

Sure.

He ran his fangs over his bottom lip. I

could taste blood in my own mouth. *Too damn late.*

And it always has been, hasn't it?

You said it, not me.

Jebediah began his opening invocation, honing the gathered psychic intensity of the coven. It rushed forward and receded like a tidal force. I saw Uriel cut off another knuckle and let it drop across the stones at his feet. There was no sign of Fane.

My lifeline kept prowling around in my hand. If I was going to make a different choice it had to be now. I didn't know what would happen if I stepped out of the circle. Any other time the invocation would be subverted and possibly backfire, causing a psychic recoil that might blind or kill any of the members. Jebediah's will swallowed us. But the spell had already gone beyond the coven. I could feel it. We weren't needed at all—Armageddon was already here, and we didn't have anything to do with it.

I stepped from the majik circle and nothing happened.

The silver light surrounding the others continued to glow, and Jebediah had thrown himself so deeply into his incantations that his eyes had rolled up into the back of his head.

Find Fane.
Why?
I don't know.
Well, that's helpful.
I think it might be important.
Now look who needs help.

I backed away and started searching the ruins for Fane. Self crept along beside me, feeling the same thing in his gut that I did. My dad started doing the Hustle and twisted into a few other disco craze dances. His rhythms started snarling in my brain. Shadows slithered together and parted around us. I thought I spotted a splash of red, a flash of pink, and a hint of steam in the chill air.

There, Self said, pointing. *She's got him.*

Fane lay on his back between two collapsed pillars, gutted but still breathing, sputtering blood from his frothing lips. He held both hands to his belly, trying to keep himself from spilling out. His stiletto lay on the ground beside him in a lake of his blood.

Self and I looked up at the same moment to see four miscarriages bobbing on silver cords overhead, their translucent, vein-heavy skin shimmering in the dark sunlight.

Another psychic cord trailed disconnected down in the dirt.

"Oh shit," I said.

Coincidence didn't exist anymore. I should've realized that I had met her on the plane for a reason.

Betty Verfenstein moved closer, holding a butcher knife, her pink hair curled into little wings from where it had been spattered with Fane's blood.

The elderly plump woman gave her defiant, rough laugh. Three days ago it had filled me with a pleasant warmth but this time it just scared the hell out of me.

Fane was trying to talk, sputtering as his belly continued to bubble up around his fingers. He stared directly at me. "Don't . . ."

I kneeled and thought about trying to console him, but Fane was in agony and I knew he enjoyed it. A martyr lives to die. "What?"

He seized hold of my arm with his dripping fist. "Don't bring me . . . back. . . ."

"I won't," I told him, and he just had time to nod thanks before he was gone.

"He was going to kill you," Betty said. "He was sneaking up on you ready to cut your throat."

I believed her, but that didn't change a

damn thing. I looked into her face more closely than I had before, and I finally noticed that she had a glass eye. My spell had worked three days ago, when I sent my curse back through time.

"Betty, it was you." My voice sounded delicate, much more frail than hers. "You murdered your own daughter."

"Sacrifices had to be made."

My mouth opened and it took me a while to get anything out. "But why?"

"I did not fail the test of Abraham."

Cool! What's your GPA?

Betty Verfenstein wasn't raving and didn't look insane. She was composed and calm and had the same air of controlled fanaticism as almost everyone else in this land of grudges. She had no more or less zeal about killing her family as the men forced to murder their loved ones and commit suicide at Masada.

"I had to keep you walking on the path, following the will of the Lord. The messiah is about to return. My daughter will sit in glory at the hand of the Father tonight, with all the martyrs, beloved and blessed above all others."

There's gonna be a full house sitting at the hands of God tonight.

Dad wandered past, playing with the floating miscarriages. Their fishlike faces peered at him and he peered back, prodding them with his fingers. The psychic cord lying in the dust had been chewed through. Theresa had learned the truth about her mother and had at last escaped the old lady.

"Who told you my name?" I asked.

"I've always known your name."

"Who told you?"

"Since I was a child I've had visions. Our meeting on the airplane, your father's face covered in foundation, and wearing his ten-gallon cowboy hat. You were a ridiculous sight. I even knew you'd put my eye out, but it had to be done. Theresa dreamed of you too."

"It makes no sense."

"It had to be done."

"But why slaughter Bethany Shiya?"

"She'd achieved the goal set out before her. You laid with her and wailed for her as God demanded. Once that was done the great harlot had to be purged. But the whore of Babylon wouldn't leave the woman's body, so she had to die. Don't look so shocked, could you really have expected anything else?"

"And Gawain? Why Gawain?"

She flinched as if struck. "That pariah! Don't speak of it. It did not belong in this world."

"He was my friend!"

Craning her neck, Betty looked over the mighty stone remains of Megiddo, watching the coven sway in harmony together, chanting. Her eyes bloomed with fear and frustration. She grew shrill. "They've already begun and you left the circle. How could you have done that? Why did you leave the circle?"

"It doesn't mean anything."

"You must fulfill your duty in helping to raise the returned messiah!"

She's working to assure the second coming of Christ? With a name like Verfenstein?

"You left the circle! You've a fate to carry out!"

"I am," I said.

"No, no, it's not supposed to happen this way. I've watched over and protected you. You must lead them. God told me!"

"I'm leaving. Whatever happens, I want no part of it."

"You fool, you damned fool!"

"Listen, lady, I'm sick of all you—"

She raised her knife and lunged for me

before I could get my hands up. She had an amazing compact strength and her leap carried her right to my throat. *Watch it!* Self shouted. He dove but only caught a few pink wisps of hair in his hands. The blade descended.

My father shoved me out of the way.

The enormous blade drove into his belly up to the hilt, and he let out a soft chuckle.

He reached out with both arms and hugged Betty Verfenstein to him, pressing his painted nose to hers. She stared wide-eyed and started letting out choked, terrified cries. He planted a kiss on her forehead, and when he finally let her go she backed up into Fane's blood, slid, and tripped over his corpse. The old lady hit the ground hard, and her head snapped back and struck the rocky terrain with the sound of steak slapped down on a butcher's block.

She was dead in less than a minute.

It was too easy a resolution.

Whoa, Self said. *That was quick.*

Dad tugged the knife from his midriff and let it fall. There was barely any blood and it didn't affect him at all as he skipped back toward the circle.

The coven hadn't noticed a thing. They were beyond such dimensions. The ceremony continued on course, the twelve members lost at the bottom of the abyss inside themselves. They'd gone too far and too deep, and now struggled to remember who they were. In order to evoke a spirit you must have complete knowledge of it and the purpose it will serve. They stood at cross-ends, ignorant and unprepared. Motes of energy poured from Jebediah's eyes and bled into the air.

The sun became as black as a sackcloth of hair and ashes. My new flesh burned once again, and at the same time I was freezing.

Elijah's fury and love for Danielle swept over me so that my skin tingled and the center of my brain rang. If she hadn't loved me I would've become just as relentless and savage. A shadow blotted out the sky and fell across the entire width of the circle. Self tugged at my wrist. I slowly turned around.

The mammoth Nephilim had mutated further. Elijah's influence and delusions had altered its colossal body into the Beast of Revelation. It no longer drooled down its massive silken neck, but instead walked grim-jawed and frowning in rage. His ire fueled the great beast with seven heads and seven horns and ten crowns. Elijah's pride had given us the Red Dragon.

Man, Self said, *that is just so nasty!*

The Nephilim's mouth still hung open in a centuries-old cry. If Elijah was still in there, then he too had mutated, and so had his hatred. Perhaps the hybrid's two hundred angelic fathers screamed in some hollow between heaven and limbo.

The body of the Beast had matured, though it was no larger than before. I could see its heart stirring, that giant chest pulsing, though the Nephilim didn't breathe. Although it had no genitalia, or at least it hadn't before, Elijah knew shame and had covered the hybrid's groin with knotted sheets and blankets and woven rugs. Its digits had fully formed now, and those massive hands were partially clenched at the Beast's sides.

The skin was no longer paler than my father's whiteface. Like my new flesh, when the Dragon climbed into the sunshine it had burned. Hills of salt adhered to its shoulders and head, powdering its face. It must have lain in the Dead Sea for some time before finally standing, one foot on land and one in the water on the lowest spot on earth, fulfilling all the prophecies Elijah intended to live out.

I think we'd better run, Self urged.

How the hell did it get here?

I don't know. It must have other minions like Uriel who helped to carry out its plans.

Uriel stared at the great Beast and didn't seem to know what it was any longer. Perhaps he'd always understood that the Nephilim would play some role at the hour of the apocalypse, but to see it standing before him in the guise of the Dragon made his tongue unfurl. His already fragile mind shattered further as he took the sword and lopped off his left arm at the elbow.

Uriel held the spurting stump up to the Dragon Elijah. "Oh Lord," he begged, "free me from thy will."

Yes, it would definitely be a good idea if we ran away now.

"The locusts," Uriel whimpered, pointing the stump to the south. "The locusts have been set upon mankind."

There shall be a hail of fire and blood, stars will darken and fall. The locusts shall be released to torment the faithless, wearing breastplates, with tails like scorpions and faces of men. A shimmering dark cloud wreathed the Nephilim's broad head, surging and alive and glittering. Thin, broad wings beat frantically and glints of metal flickered. The sound was an incredible whirring and buzzing. There were already thousands of grasshoppers gathering in force, and their eggs sifted through the air in lengthy fibers like webs. Soon millions of locusts would cover the Jezreel Valley and sweep out across all the kingdoms of the earth.

Damn, those are ugly critters! Self said.

I'd taken those passages in the Bible as a symbol of the Roman empire, soldiers who crushed the Middle East and destroyed everything in their path like locusts. But, God, how I'd been wrong.

I realized that Jebediah didn't want to raise Christ for any human purpose or intent. He'd been power mad and hungry for revenge countless times in his life, but that was over with.

Now he simply wanted to bring about the end of the world.

The coven was still entranced by their communal link, and only Marcus looked as if he might be making an effort to break free. His jaws were clenched tight and the glow around his body pulsed erratically. He didn't feel me in the circle and it was me he wanted.

Jebediah leered. He thought I was trapped with him, raising Christ or only dragging up hell, in league with him in bringing about the devastation of everything. I wanted to kill him so badly that my mouth watered. Self growled, and I growled.

Uriel bled out quickly and fell. My father mouthed words to himself and glanced over at me as though he retained his mind. Dad reached for Uriel's sword but was too weak to wield it. The heavy point dragged in the sand as he dropped before it, on his knees, his cheek pressed to the sharp edge until his blood ran over the clown makeup.

Self suddenly leaped for him with his claws outstretched, ready to disembowel my father. He took one wild swiping slash at Dad before I got in front and struggled with him.

Stop!

Listen—

Back off!

Trust me!

And I heard something in Self's voice that I had never heard before.

He was pleading with me.

And with an overpowering clarity I knew then who had brought back Griffin to burn me down to the marrow so I might be reborn. Now I understood why Griffin had shouted, "He loves you! He is your child, you are his child."

We needed trust but we didn't have it. Instead we were inextricable and eternally bound. We didn't need trust—we only needed each other.

I was his child. He was my child.

I turned and looked at my father and saw the four deep scratches in his chest and the knife wound in his belly.

I took hold of my father, who smiled as his tongue lolled. My hands began to flare— the black dazzling flash rising up my arms, the arcane flames heating the air until dust devils swept around us.

I reached into the center of my father and kept reaching, and pulled hard. My fists were on fire, but the harlequin costume wouldn't burn.

And from within my father came tiny fingers reaching out.

I gritted my teeth, grabbed hard, and hauled. I caught hold of a chubby arm and kept pulling. I yanked until a huge head like a hydrocephalic child's finally crowned, watching it slowly slide free of the flesh. My father began laughing, giving birth to this. Then came the archangel's fat face, the smooth pale shoulders, and the coarse tiny wings. Michael shook himself off like a wet dog, sneering in the midst of all heaven's enemies. His eyes rolled, bottom lip drooping, silly little wings unfolding. His misshapen head bobbed left and right.

Archangel Michael looked exhausted and stupid, or perhaps only insane.

I couldn't stop wondering who had the power to have imprisoned this great warlike prince of Seraphim this way, stuffed down inside a dead clown.

Gawain.

He must've gotten the idea from the baby hidden in Eddie's chest. I didn't comprehend how or why he did it, but I knew that I trusted Gawain more than I did Abbott John or anybody else. I tried to shove Michael's misshapen head back inside my father's chest cavity. The angel gave me a startled angry look and pulled, twisted, and heaved, working his dwarfish body free.

Self clambered up my back and screamed, *What are you doing? Let him out! Let him out!*

Someone else was there helping. I

glanced over and saw Marcus shoulder to shoulder with me. Fighting Jebediah's spell had taken its toll on him—his hair had been singed and the stink of ozone clung to him. His lips were white, and the knotted veins at his temples stood out thick and blue as nightcrawlers.

His hands pressed against Michael's face and together we grunted as we grappled with the angel. Marcus reared back and started hammering Michael in his nubby nose as I tried to fold my father's separated flesh back over the small fists, but it didn't work. We were covered in blood and watery colored fluids. Dad kept giggling and wriggling as if he found this all to be ticklish.

With a loud and nauseating sound of suction, like a shoe being pulled from a mud hole, the archangel Michael emerged covered in ropes of mucus and internal juices.

His wings barely functioned well enough to carry his stunted cherubic body awkwardly over our heads. Dad clapped and made gestures urging him to fly. Michael grunted in frustration as he tumbled through the air trying to gain control of himself. His erratic flight led him toward my father again, where the general of heaven's armies crashed into Dad and bowled him over. They both hit the ground.

I grabbed Uriel's sword and found it incredibly heavy and unwieldy. My father hopped back up on his feet and grasped the handle with me. His slashed harlequin's suit lay wet and sticking all over his chest so that I didn't have to watch his naked pink lungs working like a bellows. Self yanked Michael up by the tip of one wing and forced him forward until he touched the sword.

Instantly the metal ignited with a fire that didn't burn. Its energy made the inside of my head hum until my back teeth sang. I didn't see how Michael could possibly bring down the behemoth without us, so I gently pressured my dad in the direction of the swing and hoped we could pull it off. The Dragon had not moved at all except for its seven heads shifting in different poses, each one completely expressionless.

Marcus squinted and covered his face. The fire and Elijah's hate were too much for him, standing this close. It blanketed the area like a radiation leak or a toxic waste spill. He was still too weak to fight this kind of venom. The locusts swarmed around us, their human faces on grasshopper bodies speaking in minuscule voices I couldn't understand. Self swatted and ate them by the dozens, and Hotfoot Johnson and the black owl Prickeare did the same, soaring between the Dragon's legs and over its shoulders. Imps jumped and bounced all over, feasting. Jamara dragged itself forward grabbing mouthfuls of the locusts and spitting out their brass breastplates.

I looked up at the Dragon. *It's already dead.*

Not quite.

Elijah's not in there. He's abandoned that body. It's just a mindless hulk again. It's not the Beast of Revelation.

Perhaps it is. Or will be. We can't take any chances. We have to do these things even if they appear to be pointless.

His honesty stopped me and made me snap around to look at him. *Why?*

Self shrugged. *You got me.*

My father, Michael, and I hefted the sword together and drove it into the Dragon's gigantic ankle.

It was already a creature of stone, and as the fire from the sword moved up the Dragon's leg it seemed to absorb the crimson coloring and draw it from the beast. Once again the hybrid turned ashen, and fissures ran up the length of its marble-hewn skin. Elijah's hatred animated it now, but his soul was on the loose. Boulder-sized chunks of its body began to break free and crumble around us. We ran for cover and I dragged my dad back toward the ruins. Michael's expression was one of confusion—even he didn't believe his war with the great Red Dragon could be won so easily as this. He shook his oversize head slowly, knowing that this was only a staged Armageddon of cardboard and smoke, and that he'd been betrayed and misused.

The archangel Michael, warrior hand of God and general of all heaven's armies, turned and glared at me with such intense malice, with the infinite and eternal hate so clear and bright in his eyes, that I trembled until I almost couldn't stand any longer. He sneered and pointed at my heart, and with his little wings flapping he flew off to the south, deranged and furious.

I knew he'd be back one day for his revenge.

He wanted this. Damn him.

Who?

Elijah.

Silver glow ebbing with the coming of evening, the coven began to awaken from Jebediah's spell. The two girls pregnant with Fuceas-spawn immediately dropped inside the magik circle and began to shriek and writhe as they miscarried the hellborn.

I sat in the center of Jebediah's majik circle for the greatest focus of astral energy, tasting the hint of his remnant incantations and charms. He was still smiling and the hexes bled even faster from his eyes. I tightly crossed my legs, feet pulled up so that they touched opposite thighs, spine straight and head back. Motes of black energy leaked from my mouth and wafted past, encircling my own eyes. My hands were at the center of my chest with fingers interlaced into specific placement. Pinkies, thumbs, and index fingers steepled, and these three steeples each pointing back at myself—thumbs aimed at the heart, pointers at my throat, pinkies toward the forehead.

I looked over and Marcus was doing the same, joining me in this invocation and on this journey, wherever it might lead.

Jebediah wasn't about to quit. He intensified his spell and the chanting of the coven grew louder. Even the girls aborting on the ground were still caught in the lacework of his scheme. Their mouths spoke words while their bellies writhed and the bubbling pink yolk and eggs of the demon earl Fuceas ran out from between their legs.

I visualized his bitterness and I imagined his happiness, the same duality existing in him as in me. His chin leaked sparks and his scarred face lit with remorse, hopelessness, and the lonely intense wish for death and absolution. No wonder we had found each other. We were so much alike.

I saw his heart's desire and I would summon it. Jebediah felt my lengthy reach across the drawn veil, my will joined to Marcus's as we went beyond life and nature.

"What?" Jebediah said. "What is happening? You're doing something!"

I finally knew in my heart that he had not asked me to the place of battles in order to take over the world or do God's will or instigate Armageddon.

He only wanted me to save him.

What time is it?

The ninth hour, of course, Self said. *You know what you're doing?*

It's a little too late to ask now, isn't it?

It's always been too late.

You said it, not me.

Jebediah's hold on the others loosened and they began to rouse from their stupor.

"What is this?" he yelled, terrified because the world had not yet ended. "What are you doing!"

"I'm giving you what you want, Jebediah."

It was easy to draw power from him as his psychic lusts and ghosts, needs and dreads seethed, churned, and fermented deep within. I caught pieces of desires that weren't my own, each ripping at me like teeth and talons. The edges of my vision turned black and red. My hair stood on end and sweat drenched every inch of me. Waves of violent force pounded and twined around all of us. I spoke the necessary ancient words clearly, my tongue wrapping around the uncomfortable sounds and spitting them out. Self urged me on, shivering and trapped in the backwash of our making.

"You don't know what I want!"

"I told you once. This isn't about Christ," I said.

I summoned forth Peck in the Crown, purified and accepted into heaven.

Jebediah's familiar, his second self, dead as long as Danielle, slowly appeared before me in a maelstrom of eddying shadows and light. Dark jagged bolts of skipping energy erupted from the earth. He looked so much like Jebediah, and Self, and me, all of us there in his small dead face coming to life. He looked at me and smiled.

Peck in the Crown wandered free and looked toward Jebediah. Both of their mouths worked silently as they stumbled toward each other with open arms and embraced among us.

Marcus unwound from his position sucking air loudly and slumped onto his side, completely drained from aiding me. Dad shuffled over and peered at the stirring shadows. Something was wrong. Even though I'd ended it the spell of resurrection continued on its own.

There was another presence here, grabbing on to my will and forcing itself back onto the earth. For a moment I prayed it was Danielle, and then I was absolutely terrified that it might be her.

And from those swollen, swirling shadows of light and anguish came another.

He had eyes like a flame of fire, and his feet were of fine brass, his hair white as wool. He felt as empty and ethereal as the broken promises of heaven. I touched his hand, smooth and cold.

My mind throbbed with a rising scream

that eventually made it to my mouth. Whoever had pulled the strings today—Jebediah, Elijah, Satan, or someone else—had not counted on the will of God. Now would begin the apocalypse. A third of humanity would immediately die, the oceans boiling and turning to blood, a plague of locusts loosed on mankind as starvation and war and pestilence ran through the nurseries and yards. As the stars fell from the night sky the true Dragon would rise from the depths and begin a reign of torment, misery, and depravity that would last a thousand years.

I couldn't let it happen.

Betty's butcher knife still lay nearby in the dust. Self or I or Dad or all of us shrieked until our throats cracked.

I picked up the knife and stabbed forward into the light.

Sorrowful, sympathetic eyes gazed at me as hot blood sprayed across my hands.

"Forgive me!" I howled.

Blazing eyes, dying but not forgiving.

It was done.

Chapter Twenty

The wind blew again, rising and falling.

Jebediah wept and Peck in the Crown sobbed with him. He looked back at me over his shoulder, his face still wet with tears. "How can you be sure that what you've done is right?"

"I'll be back for Danielle's body."

"That doesn't matter now."

"It's all that matters to me."

He couldn't hide his shock. "What if this was to be the time of judgment, and your meddling has doomed the world? How can you be certain that God himself isn't seething at this? Raging and gathering all the wrath and forces of heaven to be turned against you now?"

"You just remember what I said."

Crushed and bitten-through grasshoppers lay strewn across the Plain of Esdraelon. The monolithic child of Armon now lay in broken pieces that looked no different from the rest of the ruins and sacrificial altars of Megiddo.

No one else spoke to me. Jebediah and the rest of the coven simply walked off without a word. Marcus glanced at me as if he had a great deal to say, but in the end he trudged off without saying it.

Self climbed my father's costume and worked on his chest. It took a lot of touching up but eventually he got Dad's torso back in good enough shape that nothing was hanging out.

And the great day of his wrath has come, and who shall be able to stand?

The blood of the man named Yashua had dried on my hands.

Self asked, *Now what?*

We got back into the Jaguar and sat there for a while until the moon began to rise. It was no longer a wolf's moon but now shone cold and harsh and brilliant. Dad sat contentedly in the passenger seat with his hands in his lap, twitching from time to time. I left the window down and let the breeze wash over us, bringing me back again to those days on the beach before—before—

I started the Jag and let it out, the engine going from a purr to a dull roar. I didn't know what to do next or where we were going.

It was Easter Sunday.

My father turned his dead white face to me and said, "Woo woo."

THE DECEASED
TOM PICCIRILLI

Something is calling Jacob Maelstrom back to the isolated home of his childhood—to the scene of a living nightmare that almost cost him his life. Ten years ago his sister slaughtered their brother and parents, locked Jacob in a closet . . . then committed a hideous suicide. Now, as the anniversary of that dark night approaches, Jacob is drawn back to a house where the line between the living and the dead is constantly shifting.

But there's more than awful memories waiting for Jacob at the Maelstrom mansion. There are depraved secrets, evil legacies, and family ghosts that are all too real. There's the long-dead writer, whose mad fantasies continue to shape reality. And in the woods there are nameless creatures who patiently await the return of their creator.

___4752-7 $6.99 US/$8.99 CAN

HEXES

TOM PICCIRILLI

Matthew Galen has come back to his childhood home because his best friend is in the hospital for the criminally insane—for crimes too unspeakable to believe. But Matthew knows the ultimate evil doesn't reside in his friend's twisted soul. Matthew knows it comes from a far darker place.

___4483-8 $6.99 US/$8.99 CAN

IN THE DARK

RICHARD LAYMON

Nothing much happens to Jane Kerry, a young librarian. Then one day Jane finds an envelope containing a fifty-dollar bill and a note instructing her to "Look homeward, angel." Jane pulls a copy of the Thomas Wolfe novel of that title off the shelf and finds a second envelope. This one contains a hundred-dollar bill and another clue. Both are signed, "MOG (Master of Games)." But this is no ordinary game. As it goes on, it requires more and more of Jane's ingenuity, and pushes her into actions that she knows are crazy, immoral or criminal—and it becomes continually more dangerous. More than once, Jane must fight for her life, and she soon learns that MOG won't let her quit this game. She'll have to play to the bitter end.

___4916-3 $6.99 US/$8.99 CAN